THU

ROTHERHAM LIBRARY & INFORMATION SERVICE

L752

| 1 9 NOV 2016 | 2 7 SEP 2018 | |
| 1 5 DEC 2016 | FEATHER | |
| 1 4 JAN 2017 | RAWMARSH | |
| 1 0 FEB 2017 | 2 2 APR 2023 | |
| WICKERSLEY | | |
| - 9 AUG 2018 | | |
| 1 8 AUG 2018 | | |

This book must be returned by the date specified at the time of issue as the DATE DUE FOR RETURN.
The loan may be extended (personally, by post, telephone or online) for a further period if the book is not required by another reader, by quoting the above number / author / title.

**Enquiries: 01709 336774**

**www.rotherham.gov.uk/libraries**

**The angrier she got, the pinker she got, and the more heated her whispers became...**

And, despite her tirade, with his close proximity she kept looking at his mouth as she made her displeasure known. When she did subconsciously she'd lick her lips, or for a fraction of a second lose her train of thought.

For once he had no idea how she'd respond to a kiss. Would it scare her off? Make her agree to go back to the palace and then home? Make her want more?

What reaction did he even want? He was no longer certain he could follow through on the idea to kiss her senseless and send her away for the sake of his friendship with her brother.

All his planning didn't give him what he needed. Curling his hand around that bun her hair had been worked into, he pulled her to meet him and caught her with her mouth open. A tiny sound of surprise and alarm sounded in her throat, but it took very little for her to relax into his grip. Her head fell back and it took no coaxing at all for him to gain entrance into her mouth.

Suddenly it was no longer about scaring her away. It was about the feeling that rolled over him as his hand left her hair and he wrapped his arms around her...

Dear Reader,

In my mind, there are three kinds of sheikh heroes:

1. The kind of sheikh I like.

2. The kind of sheikh I want to shake to death.

3. The hybrid sheikh—the one I want to shake to death, but who eventually wins me over by learning from his mistakes and giving me some good grovelling at the end.

Number threes are my favourite. Throw some sleep therapy into the concept, and I'm hooked. Of all the books I've written, this one's probably my favourite—maybe even surpassing my debut.

Before I got started, I got to do loads of super-fun 'research' (note the ironic quotes).

I watched every documentary on sleep and dreaming I could get my hands on. As an unrepentant nerd, this made me completely happy. ('Research.')

I read some smoking-hot sheikh books—you know…for mood. (More 'research'.)

And I spent hours naming fictional countries— something I'd never done before. It was surprisingly difficult but, like most of my brainstorming, I turned it into a fun game and then spent way too much time debating the best locations of the 'e' and the 'a'. ('e' and then 'a' won, because 'Merirach' sounded better than 'Marirech'. See? Yet more important 'research'!)

I'd say I hope you have as much fun reading Khalil and Adalyn's story as I had writing it, but that just seems impossible to me. So instead I'll say, if you get one quarter of my 'pleasuretainment', I'll consider all those hours of 'research' well worth the effort. :)

*Amalie* X0

# FALLING FOR HER RELUCTANT SHEIKH

BY
AMALIE BERLIN

All rights reserved including the right of reproduction in whole or in part in any form. This edition is published by arrangement with Harlequin Books S.A.

This is a work of fiction. Names, characters, places, locations and incidents are purely fictional and bear no relationship to any real life individuals, living or dead, or to any actual places, business establishments, locations, events or incidents. Any resemblance is entirely coincidental.

This book is sold subject to the condition that it shall not, by way of trade or otherwise, be lent, resold, hired out or otherwise circulated without the prior consent of the publisher in any form of binding or cover other than that in which it is published and without a similar condition including this condition being imposed on the subsequent purchaser.

® and TM are trademarks owned and used by the trademark owner and/or its licensee. Trademarks marked with ® are registered with the United Kingdom Patent Office and/or the Office for Harmonisation in the Internal Market and in other countries.

First published in Great Britain 2015
By Mills & Boon, an imprint of HarperCollins*Publishers*
1 London Bridge Street, London, SE1 9GF

Large Print edition 2016

© 2015 Amalie Berlin

ISBN: 978-0-263-26087-8

ROTHERHAM LIBRARY & INFORMATION SERVICES

F

B52 033 360 7

Our policy is to use papers that are natural, renewable and recyclable products and made from wood grown in sustainable forests. The logging and manufacturing processes conform to the legal environmental regulations of the country of origin.

Printed and bound in Great Britain
by CPI Antony Rowe, Chippenham, Wiltshire

There's never been a day when there haven't been stories in **Amalie Berlin**'s head. When she was a child they were called daydreams, and she was supposed to stop having them and pay attention. Now when someone interrupts her daydreams to ask, 'What are you doing?' she delights in answering, 'I'm working!'

Amalie lives in Southern Ohio with her family and a passel of critters. When *not* working she reads, watches movies, geeks out over documentaries and randomly decides to learn antiquated skills. In case of zombie apocalypse she'll still have bread, lacy underthings, granulated sugar, and always something new to read.

### Books by Amalie Berlin

### Mills & Boon Medical Romance

*Craving Her Rough Diamond Doc*
*Uncovering Her Secrets*
*Return of Dr Irresistible*
*Breaking Her No-Dating Rule*

Visit the Author Profile page at millsandboon.co.uk for more titles.

To Laurie Johnson, my second editor.
She once suggested I tackle a sheikh book,
something I hadn't considered before and
probably wouldn't have considered for a good
long while without her planting the seed.

To Laura McCallen, my current editor,
for supporting my tendency to run around
naked in public. Okay, that's a lie.
But she does support my tendency to go off
on wild story tangents, something
I'm extremely grateful for.

**Praise for
Amalie Berlin**

'A sexy, sensual, romantic, heartwarming and
purely emotional, romantic, bliss-filled read.
I very much look forward to this author's next
book and being transported to a world of pure
romance brilliance!'

—*Goodreads* on
*Craving Her Rough Diamond Doc*

# CHAPTER ONE

BOBBING ON WHIPLASH desert winds, Dr. Adalyn Quinn's helicopter dropped and paused, dropped and paused, descending in the aeronautical equivalent of two steps forward, one step back, each jostle adding another crack to her already brittle nerves.

Digging her nails into her seat base, she pitched forward, stiff and straining against the seat belts across her hips and torso. The overly snug belts, while uncomfortable, felt illogically safer than wobbling about like week-old gelatin, as she had been.

Her older brother tried but had never quite understood the cold, black pit of fear that sank in her middle when she even thought of travel, so there was no way for him to comprehend the abyss that had been trying to swallow her sanity during the long hours of this godforsaken journey. The one he'd tossed her into.

He'd thought himself helpful when he'd said, "Take those antianxiety medicines you never take, to help your trip."

Because remaining calm while dying a fiery death? So much better than feeling acute terror without pharmacological filters. Sure, she could concede that point. But having her wits artificially addled when she'd probably need them to escape burning, twisted wreckage—supposing she lived that long? Less brilliant.

The idea that one of the vehicles *wouldn't* crash was the thought that sounded like fantasy. Naturally, her airborne catastrophe would happen on this last leg of her trip, worlds away from lace balconies and her safe, quiet life.

Her stomach curdled as they fell another few feet. She just had to hold on a little while longer.

The pilot's voice crackled in her headphones, alerting her to their landing at the former airport site for the Kingdom of Merirach. As if she couldn't feel it. As if every shift of the wind didn't brutalize her mind with images of crashes and broken, twisted bodies. After nearly twenty-four hours of this self-inflicted mental torture it would be easy to think she'd become numbed to it, but that primal fear still had the ability to tighten her body until her shoulders stretched stiffly, like old boot leather. She wouldn't have been surprised if at any second her skin cracked and her collarbone snapped in half.

Broken.

Twisted.

Body.

They touched down with a jolt, bounced twice and settled. She immediately began fumbling with the latches on her belts, trying to get free. To get out of the flying death trap. To get to him.

Adalyn had a rule about putting her life or well-being into someone else's hands. A simple rule really...*don't do it!* But right now it comforted her to think that the distance between her and safety could be measured in feet. He'd be waiting for her.

Jamison's best friend.

The one she'd never met because she didn't travel, but to whom Jamison had sent her.

He'd be there, and he'd take her to a nearby hotel where she could eat the protein bars she'd brought for sustenance, drink water purified by her special tablets and sit in the dark with the earplugs she'd brought to create the illusion of solitude.

She could rest. Sleep. Sleep was what she needed. Sleep and alone time somewhere without wheels attached. If she had all that, it might lower her blood pressure enough that she couldn't see her clothing move from the force of each beat of her heart...

"Door," she said, dragging the headphones off and hanging them from the armrest on her seat. And then again, "Door."

Why were they moving so slowly?

She needed out.

Tomorrow she would officially see her patient, work on diagnosing and outlining a treatment plan, then go the heck home.

End of adventure.

The only thing she had going for her now was the darkened interior of the helicopter. No one could see her expression. She didn't have to work so hard to keep it all hidden as she had on the other planes and vehicles. The last thing she wanted was to put her issues on display and have someone label her hysterical—one of the most offensive words she'd ever learned and had heard daily in the months after the crash.

Outside the chopper, in the not-too-far distance, a ring of headlights provided the only light source, aside from the blinking things on the helicopter controls. Even she—the Queen of Never Ever Traveling—knew what an airport looked like at night. Runways. Dual bands of lights. A big building with lots of people inside. Lots of light.

Here there was only darkness and the cars. One more dangerous vehicle for her to climb into before she reached her assignment.

It really wasn't any wonder that someone living in a country so recently torn apart by civil war would have sleep difficulties, but she was here anyway.

Seconds later, the door slid open and a blast of cold air surprised her lungs, sending her into a coughing fit. But with the help of her black-suited entourage, she still scrambled from the helicopter. Once her feet hit solid ground she hunched forward and ran toward the cars, clueless as to whether or not the men followed.

Only when she reached the cars, far outside the reach of the rotating blades of death, did she straighten and look back. Two of her escorts—men in suits who'd met her at the airport of the neighboring kingdom—had made the run with her and the rest now gathered her embarrassing amount of luggage and followed.

Should she tip them? Was that expected? Insulting? Her travel book had said nothing about how to treat the servants of a royal house.

The man who had been her translator reached her side and herded her toward one of several identical sport utility vehicles with darkened windows. Though he was careful not to touch her, he wrenched open the back door of the vehicle and gestured to her with such force that she climbed in.

Unlike when he'd retrieved her, the man didn't even attempt English this time. With so little sleep and such a terrible grasp of the language, Adalyn couldn't even tell where the words started and stopped in whatever he'd said. He could've even said one of the couple of hundred words she'd managed to learn, and she wouldn't have known it.

How much farther would they have to go?

Once she stopped moving, her body caught up with her lungs—recognizing the cold finally— and she folded her arms across her chest and rubbed them to try to increase their warmth.

"You should've worn a jacket."

The low male voice broke through the sound of her pounding heart and shivering breaths, the first indication she wasn't alone in the car. She turned and as her eyes adjusted to the low lighting after the blinding headlights she could make out a traditionally robed figure not two feet away in the seat beside her.

"I thought I was coming to a hot place. I was told that it was chilly at night, but I thought that just meant I needed long sleeves, not a parka."

A soft sound—trapped somewhere between a sigh and a chuckle—answered her. Like strained amusement.

"Are you Khalil?" *Please, say yes.* She'd made

it all the way to his country—surely he would meet her at the airport?

Loud voices outside the vehicle cut through the air and her fellow passenger's voice dropped to a sharp whisper. "Yes. We will speak further at the palace, Adalyn. It isn't far."

"Palace? I thought we would be working in a clinic environment. And I'd stay at a hotel."

"I do not sleep at a clinic."

"Right… Sorry…" Of course he wouldn't sleep at a clinic. Why had she thought that? Because it was familiar. Because that's how things worked where she practiced…at her clinic. But this place was not New Orleans.

"Later I will explain." His words clipped the frosty air with short, abrupt sounds. If she could still see her breath, his words would've probably floated away in blocky cubes, formed by hard right angles and razor edges.

The front car doors opened, the suited men climbed in and for seconds she could see him under the light of the dome, but he'd already turned away, cutting off the conversation with body language. It was a technique she often used, or had used enough to recognize it.

He fixed his gaze out his window, though at what she couldn't guess. Nothing, unless he had the night vision of a cat.

The status of her rescue mission suddenly seemed like a charade, as capricious and dangerous as a ride in anything with wheels. Like the large vehicle she was in. It started rolling and banished all other thoughts from her mind—just as cars always did for her. Even now, years later, having to ride in a car felt like a forced march to her own execution.

The only thought that stayed with her as she analyzed every bump and turn for the telltale feeling of a wreck in progress was: What had Jamison gotten her into?

It couldn't have been more than a couple of miles' travel, but it took ages. By the time they stopped, her jaw hurt from clenching and she felt just a little light-headed from her breathercise.

Khalil climbed out as soon as the vehicle stopped rolling, before Adalyn could even really get a glimpse of him. "See her settled in the suite adjoining mine." All she could make out was a tall man with dark robes and the traditional dress that by turns intrigued and worried her.

Once those words were out—and in English, no less—he immediately switched over to his native tongue, leaving no doubt that he wasn't speaking to her. Well, the sooner she got to her suite, the sooner she could sleep and, she prayed, stop shaking…

Khalil tugged on a clean shirt. A dress suit. At this hour… Since he'd been in Merirach, he hadn't worn much but the robes, at least when he was in the palace and bound to the demands of his position, but Western dress would probably set her more at ease.

If he was honest, it was more than that. The robes that tradition dictated reminded him what he was doing there, and the responsibility he carried. Of who he was supposed to be. Not himself. But now, dealing with her, he didn't want to be Sheikh Khalil of Akkari, Regent of Merirach, he wanted to be Dr. Khalil Al-Akkari—the son not born to rule. Maybe it would help them both deal with the situation if they came at it as equals.

Tomorrow he'd have to go back to the robes that helped people in his host kingdom identify him as the current regent, and she'd have to become used to seeing him in them.

Knowing Jamison's history meant he knew the history of his chubby little sister, too. Jay always referred to her as the world's biggest introvert. A homebody who considered a trip to the library or bookstore to be her portal to all things exotic. Anyone would be leery of traveling to a country so recently out of a civil war, but someone who never traveled—not even on the best of circumstances—compounded the size of the favor he'd owe her for agreeing to come such a long way to help him out.

It was late so he skipped the tie—he wanted familiarity, not formality. Just to be courteous.

The other courteous thing would've been to send one of the family jets to retrieve her, at least then she would've arrived sooner and had an easier journey, but that would've just triggered questions from his elder brother. Malik always had questions. The sort of questions Khalil had no desire to answer. And if things worked out with Adalyn, questions he'd never have to answer.

He stepped through the door to the adjoining room where she'd been settled, and froze in his tracks. Her back was to him, all supple skin on display, so pale he'd swear she'd never even heard of the sun. The only thing covering her was a scrap of white cotton panties stretched over the plump little cheeks on display as she bent over the bed and dug around in the suitcase for clothes.

She'd had the same idea to change.

She just hadn't been as quick about it as he had.

She really wasn't the chubby little girl he'd seen in pictures…

Khalil's mouth watered so sharply that his jaw ached.

He swallowed, shocked by the pang of want that shot through him.

Smooth, slender and curved…she looked like a cool, life-giving oasis in a barren landscape.

Not yet aware that he'd entered, she continued

by straightening with another scrap of white cotton she shook out and pulled over her head.

Khalil closed his eyes, a baby first step that allowed him a small measure of control of his body, control he needed to force a half turn away from her. When he knew he'd be facing the wall, he opened his eyes again, but he could still see her in his peripheral vision.

*Damn.*

He closed them again. It was either that or give in to the powerful urge to look. Clearing his throat was the best warning he could think of to soften the surprise of his arrival. "I apologize, I should've knocked."

She squawked and then there was a thump, along with some other commotion he couldn't identify. If it had taken effort to look away, it took even more not to look back.

"Should I come back?" he asked, because he had to do something…

"Yes!" The word erupted from her and set him in motion. As he reached for the door, a more tentative babble came from behind him, "No, wait. You can stay, just don't turn around for a minute."

She muttered something beneath her breath, disgruntled words he couldn't make out. If she was anything like her brother, those words wouldn't be fit for company anyway.

Khalil stayed in place and stared hard at the carved wooden door.

Count the lines in the wood grain.

Don't think of the mostly nude woman behind him.

And for God's sake, don't look.

He lost track of the lines and had to start again. Keeping control of his mind and actions was easier when he wasn't tired, but he'd been in the palace for nearly a week this time around... *Tired* wasn't a strong enough word for what he was— he was exhausted in a way that even heart-accelerating doses of caffeine couldn't help.

"You can turn around. I guess I'm decent." She didn't sound at all certain.

When he turned back, it was to overly bright eyes and pink cheeks. He locked his gaze to hers in another effort to exert control over his baser impulses. "You don't look like your picture…" Which was not the way he'd intended to start this conversation.

"Sorry."

Why was she apologizing? He was the one who'd barged in.

She tugged at the bottom hem of her short dressing robe, the fidgeting making clear her response: sorry was a verbal fidget.

In the picture he'd seen, she'd been at least thirty pounds heavier and the victim of an unfortunate complexion issue. She'd worn glasses and had kept her hair pulled back in a haphazard ponytail. She'd looked like someone studious and intelligent. And now…she looked like a dark-haired pixie with large green eyes. And breasts he could clearly see the shape of through the slinky blue material of her robe.

*Eyes! Look at her eyes!*

He'd had a reason to come into the room…

"Your equipment…" He grasped for his train of thought.

She clutched the robe tighter, eyes widening further as her voice hitched. "My equipment?"

"Not that equipment…" It was all he could do not to groan at yet another verbal misstep. It didn't help that he'd put her one door away from him, like a shiny-new mistress. And, sweet mercy, did she ever look the part of timid virgin, blushing and stammering the first time her body was exposed to a man's eyes.

For the first time in Khalil's life he wished he could take advantage. Tear that robe off her, coerce and tease until she lay back on the thick bed behind her…and welcomed him with open arms. And legs. His eyes wandered down, past the hem of the silky material to the smooth, pale, shapely legs…

*For God's sake, look her in the eye.*

"My men have brought your *medical* equipment to the palace." He cleared his throat, which had gone dry again. "Where would you like it delivered?"

"Oh." She shifted around again, fidgeting with the belt and the hem again, anywhere the material folded or covered her. "I assumed that I was placed in this room so that I would have access to your room to monitor you as you sleep."

With a quick hop—which sent too many interesting places jiggling—she rounded the suitcase
and perched on the corner of the bed. Her knees
clamped together and she resumed smoothing the
fabric down her thighs, willing it to cover more
of her body than it had when she'd been standing. "Monitors here, but the camera equipment
in your room. I know that sounds really creepy,
but it is recorded so I can review it the next day
to make sure that I didn't miss anything, but
after that it gets erased. Otherwise I'd just have
to hover at your bedside and watch you sleep."

A short nervous laugh escaped her before she
clamped her lips shut, the very picture of distress despite the laugh. "I doubt anyone would be
able to get any rest if they felt like someone was
standing there, leering at them. My aunt's cat
used to do that in the morning when she wanted
me up. Just sit there and stare… And it always
worked. Woke me right up."

Babbling, a sign of nerves. Definitely nervous.
Maybe shy, too, if the way she worked to keep
him from even seeing her knees was anything

to go by. And all that wasn't what he should be focusing on.

He'd known she would need to monitor him, he was familiar with the method in which sleep studies were conducted, but the way she described watching him sleep only made him think of that long dark hair spread across cool white cotton pillows…and the slinky robe slipping over pale, soft flesh.

She added, "It'll take several hours to set up all the equipment so I thought maybe we would do it tomorrow. I really won't be of any use to anyone until I've had at least eight hours."

Right, she was tired. He should say something, stop her babbling.

"Of course."

Had he ever dated a woman so shy and modest? If he had, he should probably remember her if that appealed to him so much. He'd think less of any man who confessed this sort of reaction to innocence. To think himself capable of it. That emotion could be named by the taste of bile at the back of his throat.

But the sudden, intense aversion to the thought of accepting her help disgusted him even more.

Help was the whole reason for her to be there. He should just tell her everything right now. That would replace the sweet, nervous innocent with something uglier, a reflection of the blackness devouring him from the inside out. She'd give him her pity, at best, and she sure as hell wouldn't sit there, barely clothed, trusting him to fake his way through the actions of a good man.

"I doubt the equipment is going to be very helpful. My problem is I don't sleep. I've got insomnia. And when I fail to fall asleep, I don't tend to stay in bed for hours, trying. Not a lot to monitor when that happens. Which happens a great deal of the time." He'd opened his mouth, said words, but not the right ones. His throat refused to let those words pass.

"Well, you have to sleep sometime. I mean, you're not a drooling idiot right now, and after you miss enough sleep—well, I'm sure you've noticed the effects. But there are also other effects that are actually quite dangerous. We all have a maximum amount of time we can go without sleep and then our brains start taking micro-sleeps when we're trying to work. Or trying to drive. Insomnia sounds like a pain in the butt, but really it can be very dangerous."

Dangerous, like his reaction to her. "So your solution to it is?"

Solution? The only one he needed right this second was the one that would keep him from ogling his oldest friend's little sister.

"There are a lot of different treatments, and sometimes that means a sleeping pill if you're at a state where it's gotten very dangerous for you to stay awake."

He'd never consciously liked the idea of innocence before. Before he'd come into the room and been tantalized by the nearly nothing she'd had on—coupled with his weakened state—this was certainly a natural reaction. Not just another flaw in his character.

"Lose this battle so you can live to keep fighting the war. On another day. Night."

He just had to remember who she was and what she was to him. It shouldn't matter to him what she thought of him, so he should be able to tell

Adalyn the truth and actually get the help he'd dragged her around the globe for, not send her to treat imaginary illness.

"You know," she continued, "if the battle is a desire to sleep the natural way. Sleep aids aren't the greatest thing in the world, but sometimes they are necessary as you're trying to retrain yourself and your bed habits." She yawned, reminding him that she was tired, too. Probably jet-lagged.

And she'd stopped smoothing her robe closed. Definitely tired.

He remained standing as stiff as his suit by the door. "I have sleep aids but, as you said, I try not to use them. I may have dragged you across the world for nothing, Dr. Quinn." Doctor. Not Adalyn. Speak to her professionally, and perhaps his thoughts would follow that lead.

"Am I getting that you don't want me to be here? Did Jamison twist your arm into agreeing to this?" Her gaze sharpened and she stood, her head tilting and those pretty green eyes fixing on him with an intensity that faked alertness. And a little bit of hope. "Because if you really don't want me here, we could take a day or two and just diagnose and prescribe a treatment and I could go home, rather than sticking around to see you through whatever you need to get right. Jamison could be satisfied with that."

"It's not that I don't want you here," he said before it became clear she was offering him an out. She didn't want to be there any more than he wanted her there. They could put on a brief show of his treatment, enough to satisfy Jay, and then she would happily go home. "I just don't sleep well at the palace. Or at all. I sleep…" He rubbed his brow, pausing as he paced to a chair and sat. Her fatigue amplified his own. "I sleep better when I'm not in the palace."

"Do you keep an apartment somewhere else? Or are you referring to before you came to this kingdom to do the regent thing?"

"I don't keep an apartment. It's a tent." Why was he telling her this? Letting her witness his trouble would lead to questions, the bane of his existence. The prospect of her finding out seemed worse than the whole world finding out, and he couldn't even bring himself to care how sexist that seemed to him—not wanting to be treated or rescued by the sweet creature his inner caveman salivated over. He didn't want her to know any of it, his weakness, his shame.

"I take short medical missions out into the desert to treat those who live in camps far from medical assistance. I'm a doctor, it is just who I am, and I want to hold on to that part of myself while I'm doing my duty for my country and my family, and not let my skills grow rusty for lack of use, as they would if I stopped practicing and became a full-time bureaucrat."

"And when you're on your medical missions in a tent, you sleep better?" she said, fixating on that part.

What she should be fixating on was the fact that he didn't sleep here in the palace. If she were to continue to treat him, she'd have to go, too. "I can't explain it, but I should've thought about that before you came all this way. I know you have no desire to come out into the desert with me, and the equipment would be useless there anyway. Apologies, Adalyn."

She sat back down on the edge of the bed,

thoughtful frown firmly in place. "How long are the missions?"

"Many days." Not that many, but more than two. He would disappear for weeks on end if he could get away with it.

"And people don't know you're doing this?"

She should sound less interested, not more.

"I keep a small staff here, and I'm always available via satellite phone. Since this is not my home country—it's my mother's kingdom— the people here, especially those out in the desert camps, don't know what I look like. I go by a different name. We have a fake logo sprayed onto the trucks. It's…"

"Tricky." She grinned as she said the word and then yawned wider than she had before. "Well, I have a theory about the sleeping in the tent thing. But if you only take a short trip when you go, I'm assuming it's fairly frequent short trips?" She stopped, shifted on the bed some more and tried again. "I can go…on one trip. And that would be a few days of monitoring when you're actually sleeping. And then we can tell Jamison that we worked on a treatment plan for you to implement."

"The sun is brutal, Adalyn. You will burn to a crisp. And the heat, if you're unused to it…"

"Where I live it gets very hot. And humid. Super-humid. So humid that mold is a massive problem. I can handle heat. And wear sunblock. We'll be going in a vehicle anyway, right? Something with a roof?" She frowned momentarily, eyes sliding to the side beneath pinched brows. That was the kind of look he wanted from her. Uncertainty.

Uncertainty her words did not share. "I can go from the vehicle to the tent and not have to be in direct sunlight too much." She stood and wandered toward him but passed by to reach for the doorknob. "I hate to kick you out of a room in your home, but I'm really very tired. I think I have jet lag. Jamison never adequately described it to me before. It's awful."

He took the hint and rose to move that way. "The way my schedule is arranged, I really should head out in the morning." Before she had time to rest up.

She opened the door and held it patiently for him. "What time?"

"It's best to travel in the morning, before the heat of the day."

"What does that translate to in numbers?"

"Six to ten, give or take."

She looked at the clock, no doubt calculating just how few hours of rest she'd be getting if she actually went through with the plan. "Okay. I'll be ready at six." Another yawn and then she wandered back to the bed, leaving him at the door. "Try to rest if you can. We'll start tomorrow."

Pulling down the blankets, she crawled in—robe and all—and reached for the clock to set it.

She'd never go. In the morning, after she'd had a few hours to reset her brain and remember how much she hated to travel, she'd come to her senses and he could trundle her back off to the helicopter pad and send her home. "Good night, Adalyn. Thank you for being willing to try."

"No offense, Khalil, but I did it for Jamison. I'm sure you're a nice man and that you deserve help—it's torture to be kept awake, like real torture, and I wouldn't wish it on anyone—but if anyone else had asked me to come, you'd be on your own."

She clicked off the light and he allowed himself a tiny smile. He'd probably do anything for Jamison, too; he was closer than Khalil's real brothers had ever been. "Duly noted. And you have tried to do that by coming all the way here to meet with me."

"I'll see you at six," she said again, then sat up so he could see her only by the light spilling through the door to his chamber. "And, Khalil? Knock first next time. I wouldn't want to cause you years of therapy."

What did that mean? She'd already lain back down and burrowed into the pillow, effectively shutting him out. "Sleep well, little sister," he murmured, shutting the door behind him. Calling her "Doctor" hadn't done anything for his libido. Maybe calling her "little sister" would be able to keep him from thinking about the lush flesh he'd seen on display.

Jay needed a talk about sending his innocent, pretty little sister off to foreign countries and men who might take advantage of her.

Men of weaker constitution than Khalil.

# CHAPTER TWO

COLLEAGUES LIKED TO JOKE that Adalyn had chosen sleep medicine as her specialty in a direct reaction to how badly she'd longed for sleep during medical school and residency.

'Sleep is for the weak' was practically a motto of the twenty-first century. A crutch to help people get by in this competitive world and all its requirements for productivity, to prove they weren't beholden to the hours of vulnerability almost every living creature had to succumb to daily. The concept of sleep as a luxury.

Sacrificing sleep meant compromising health. Physical. Mental. Emotional. And she was doing it again in order to keep up with Khalil's schedule and not let her brother down. Her brother, who would want her to be healthy! Ah, more contradictions of modern living.

Sleep-deprived, but clean, mostly upright and

dressed—unlike the last time she'd seen Khalil—
Adalyn knocked on the door to his suite while
looking at her watch. Ten to six—she was tired
and only passably functioning, but she'd made
his hour of departure. She'd even managed to
pack a small bag with the bare minimum she'd
need for three days in the desert.

No answer.

He'd said he never slept in the palace, though
she doubted that was true unless he had been
out in the desert as recently as a couple of days
ago. Being tired could explain his forgetting to
knock before he'd entered her bedroom the previous night, but if he'd gone more than forty-eight
hours without any sleep he wouldn't be nearly as
coherent as he had been in their short conversation. But if he was sleeping in after she'd managed to get up and get ready…

He'd been so adamant he wouldn't sleep.

Truly, insomnia wasn't what she'd expected
she was coming to treat. One of the ways that
Jamison had talked her into coming, his stron-
gest method, had been guilt. What did you do
when a hero was wounded? You treated them.

And by the story he'd told, with bold strokes, Jamison had painted Khalil as a wounded hero. Not two months ago the country had been in revolt, the royals murdered, except for the heir—who was underage and too young to take the throne. Khalil and his brother had undertaken a mission to rescue the boy and the brother hadn't made it back. But Khalil had, with the boy—the heir who was too young to rule and now away at some school somewhere.

After all that? Well, if she'd had to guess, she'd have said his problem would've been nightmares. But then again, that was her specialty.

If he'd heard her knock, plenty of time had passed for him to throw pants on and answer the door. Adalyn knocked again. Still no answer.

Well, two knocks were warning enough. She grabbed her bag—the smallest she'd brought—and marched into Khalil's bedroom suite.

Coming from a bright room to a dark one, all she could see was the outline of heavy drapes over the bedroom windows. She couldn't even begin to guess where light switches would be in the chamber, so she marched to one of the windows and pulled open the heavy brocade curtain. And then she could see. Empty. Khalil wasn't sleeping in. Khalil wasn't there.

But at least now she could see the door leading out.

He'd all but screamed last night that he didn't want her there. She'd just expected that once they made a plan he would stick with it. Propelled by the sick feeling she'd been left, she hurried out of the room, just shy of a run.

For once her travel paranoia had done something good for her—despite her exhaustion, when the men had marched her to the suite, she'd still been able to memorize the route out of the palace in case of another sudden civil war—who knew how often those things happened in this place? Or fire. Fire was something she'd want to be able to escape without a map or a guide. One turn, another long hallway, more gilded opulence and crystal light fixtures…doors, doors, doors… another turn. She finally made it to a courtyard, having passed not a single person along the way, and stepped out just in time to see two large trucks pulling away.

Not knowing what else to do, she shouted, "Khalil!"

He sat in the driver-side window of the first truck, and when she'd shouted the name she probably shouldn't even be using at the palace he did nothing but make eye contact with her through the side-view mirror. He'd heard her but didn't take his foot off the gas.

A surge of frustration rode a wave of irritation, and before she even knew it she'd broken into a dead run after the truck.

Leaving without her? Make her travel all the way to this place, make her lose sleep and get on dangerous vehicles on land and air and then abandon her where she could be of no help to him, for no danged reason? If they made travel guide recommendations for the perfect time to shout at or make rude gestures at a royal, this would be at the top.

The trucks moved slowly enough in the court-yard to give the illusion that she might catch up with them, but the closer the gate came, the more that hopeful thought evaporated.

Muttering expletives under her breath wasn't enough, either.

The trucks slowed, making a sharp turn for the gate—too far to reach, and what was she going to do if she got there? Climb on a moving vehicle? Yeah, right.

She'd never been moved to violence by anyone before, but she dropped her bag and grabbed the nearest rock—small enough to throw but big enough to express her frustration—and channeling her anger she let the rock fly with as much force as a really tired nerdy chick could muster.

She didn't aim for him. She didn't really aim. She probably couldn't aim if she tried, at least not beyond the general intention to hit the truck somewhere, but the rock sailed strong and true, impacting the side window of the rear seat of the truck, right behind where Kahlil sat. It immediately spiderwebbed.

That stopped the truck.

That stopped both trucks.

Khalil got out, looked at the window and slammed his door. A couple tiny fragments of glass in the center of the impact rattled and fell out from the force of his gesture. He shook his head minutely at the men in the truck behind and stormed toward Adalyn, red crawling up his neck and over his face. "What the hell was that?"

Right then Adalyn remembered that she was pretty much afraid of everything. Including confrontation. Having big angry men yell at her was also on her Do Not Do list.

But if she backed down now, he'd probably just send her back inside and go on his merry way to wherever he was going.

"Emergency call button." Adalyn's short words came out with a grunt, the sound of exertion… mental if not physical. Before he reached her she jogged for the other side of the trucks to the passenger-side door. As she wrenched it open and climbed the running board to step in, strong hands locked on her hips and set her back on the ground.

There, in the relative seclusion of the side door area, he gave her a spin and forced her to face him. He was close. Too close, all but plastering her to the side of the truck, his arms forming a cage around her that kept her in place so he could effectively loom over her. "I know how you Quinns are fond of bucking authority figures, but in this country—and while still at this palace—you can't behave like that toward me."

It hit her how he was dressed. No robes today. No suit, either. He wore khakis and a light linen shirt with the collar unbuttoned, something that made him look almost like a normal person, not the autocrat he sounded like.

Their cozy little passenger-door alcove blocked the early-morning breeze and cocooned her in a heady scent of cedar, hints of citrus and something utterly masculine. Looking up into his golden-brown eyes, she felt entirely too vulnerable suddenly, as if he'd see the white flag waving in her pupils and know how close she was to backing down. She squinted at him, relying on the decreased area to make her intentions harder to read. And if it worked, she'd have to remember to use it the next time she got the harebrained idea to yell and throw rocks at a royal.

And she still couldn't hold his gaze.

Looking at his mouth? That was just as bad, but for more confusing reasons.

Her gaze tracked farther down. His neck was safe, though a vein stood out there, pulsing, and seeing how fast his heart beat caused a little flutter in her belly. Even in her worst imaginings related to this trip, they had all been about accidents, explosions and possibly drowning at sea after a water crash… Never once had she thought she'd have to fight her patient to be able to treat him. The small amount of backbone she'd found quickly faded. All she wanted to do was get her bag and go back inside, but she muttered, "You were leaving me behind on purpose."

Khalil dropped his arms and stepped back, needing to put some distance between himself and the woman who was supposed to be sleeping through his departure. Distance would help him keep from shaking some sense into her or just putting his hands back on her.

Even after he'd grabbed places on the truck and forced himself to focus on her, his palms still tingled with the memory of firm, curvy hips.

With a slow breath in through his nose, he took a few seconds to look over the courtyard. At least no one but the small private crew who traveled into the desert with him had witnessed the rock showdown.

"I assumed you wouldn't want to go." That was true, at least until he'd seen her outside with the overnight bag. After that, he really had no clue why he hadn't stopped. Maybe the idea that one more hurdle would make her give up… Only, it hadn't.

She looked him in the eye again, but he could tell from the color in her cheeks and the way her hands now gripped the door frame that her bravery was faltering. "I told you I would come last night."

"Yes, and then you had a little time to sleep on it and think more clearly. At least, I'd hoped that would be the case." He managed to calm his voice when he said it, a small victory considering he wanted to shout, *Go back inside. Go home. Go anywhere else.*

"So you really don't want me here. You let me come all this way and…" As she spoke, her words came more and more slowly, and those soft green eyes he'd so admired hardened to bare slits. She might be tired, she might not enjoy confrontation and she might be a little intimidated by him, but she was still angry. "I'm not at my best today, but I do still have a little bit of functioning gray matter working for me. You're sabotaging this on purpose."

"Adalyn—"

"No. I'm the one talking now!" She released the frame of the door and reached up to jab him once in the chest. "You didn't just let me come all this way, you assured that I would have the roughest trip possible, right? You have loads of planes—you and Jamison have gone to practically as many countries as the Peace Corps on them—but I had to arrange transport and ship the equipment…and all that. You sent your black-suited henchmen to retrieve me at the last possible minute, but that's it. You made my journey as hard as you could possibly make it in order to make me be the one who broke a promise to my brother. Didn't you?"

And he wouldn't defend it or deny it.

But if she poked him in the chest again, he was going to…

No, there would be no feeling up his best

friend's irritating little sister. He crossed his arms to keep his hands under control and said instead, "You really want to go into the desert? It's nothing like you read in books. No rest stops between here and where we're going. Poisonous creatures that sting and bite. Dust, sun, heat— this isn't some glorified field trip."

She stepped up on the running board and turned to face him, now somewhat closer to eye level, and used that added height to glare at him, her chin tilting to match the challenge in her posture. "Say it," she demanded, the tiniest wobble in her voice breaking through his resistance more than the bravado she put on. "Tell me I can't go. I'll tell Jamison that I did all I could, but, whatever you promised him, you broke your word. Go ahead, Khalil. Tell me I can't go. I'm happy to go pack my bags and find a way out of your gilded palace in the sand and go home. But you have to say it, because I came all this way for Jamison, and I'm not going to be the one who lets him down."

*Son of a...*

"Just sit down and shut up already," he muttered, shaking his head.

Adalyn drew a deep, satisfied breath, and at the second her lungs felt filled to capacity the true meaning of her victory pushed the air back out again in a rush. She'd just had a fight in order to be *allowed* to ride out into the scorching desert in a big dangerous truck with a man who really didn't want her with him.

So not a victory.

She edged onto the seat and closed the door. He rounded the truck and climbed back in at the driver's side, slamming his own door and bringing down another shard of glass from the window she'd broken and that now had a tiny hole in the center. The window that now looked...really dangerous.

"Aren't we going to change to a truck without a broken window?"

"No. Want to change your mind and go back inside?" He pulled on his seat belt and started the truck.

*Yes!*

"No, I'm going with you unless you order me

not to." And now that she thought about it, that was a really stupid idea.

The trucks started rolling forward, continuing on… Without her bag! "Are we going to turn around and fetch my bag?"

If she'd eaten anything in the past several hours, she'd have been sick. No bag meant no protein bars, no water purification tablets… She was going out into the desert where they probably only had water sources of questionable cleanliness…

"No. Want to change your mind?"

Yes. *Yes.*

"Is that all you can say?" She grit her teeth and fixed her gaze in front of her. "I'm coming with you. But if I start to stink in the next couple of days I'm going to roll around in your fresh clean clothes so you can bask in my stench just as much as I'll have to."

"Good. Someone as irritating as you are shouldn't smell so good."

The urge to take off one shoe so she could better beat him with it nearly overwhelmed her limping self-control. Yet more evidence that being sleep-deprived in a foreign land brought out the worst in her.

Could someone get motion sickness if they were only going a few miles per hour? Her stomach thought so. "You're the one who's all sultan-like, but I wouldn't think it kingly to tuck tail and run when confronted with a problem. You *should* put off your trip and stay home to get treatment."

"Amazingly enough, this isn't just something I can put off. I'm not going into the desert because you don't want me to. I'm also not going just because I'm tired and want to sleep, though honestly I am really looking forward to that part. In the other truck is a cool box with vaccinations to be given. The tribes don't have the best access to clean water, and though we've put measures into motion to change this they still struggle with disease because of it."

Okay, that deflated her anger balloon a little. Except that bit about the unclean water, and her not having the tablets… "Maybe not, but you're not going to get my bag because you want to put me out. So don't get too smug and superior just because you have a valid reason for going on this trip."

She pretended he hadn't said she smelled good, because she really didn't know what to do with that information. Thank him? Give him the name of her favorite perfume?

"Fine." He grabbed the radio handset and said something she didn't understand as the truck rolled on.

The other truck hadn't yet passed through the gate, and she turned to look over her shoulder, trying to work out what he'd just done. "Why did you agree to my coming in the first place if you're so all fired against it?"

"I was tired, Jay was persistent," Khalil answered, hanging the radio handset back in its place.

With how stringently he wanted her to not go with him, Adalyn had no illusion he would wait if she climbed out of the truck and ran to pick up her bag. Resigned, she dragged on her seat belt.

Looking at him made her angrier. Looking out the side window made her feel sick. Looking out the front terrified her. She went with angry and twisted slightly under the confines of her overly tightened seat belt to look at Khalil.

Even scowling, as he was, he was handsome. That probably played into his privileged air. Royalty, doctor, handsome… It all added up to *spoiled* and used to getting what he wanted. He probably had insomnia because his bed was too lumpy, like the princess and the pea.

"I don't buy it," she said, trying to ignore the way her stomach squeezed and rolled with every creak and crackle from the window she'd broken. The wind tore at the shards, barely holding together. What if the bits flew up and got in his eyes and blinded him and he crashed them into something deadly? She chanced another glance back at the hole, mentally calculating what was safest—for the windows up front to be up or down. If she rolled down her window, would the air flow drag the shards into the cab or push them out of the truck rather than in? Maybe they wouldn't fly around at all. Maybe this was just another paranoid scenario playing out in her mind, like the thousands of fiery deaths she'd imagined on the way there.

*Stay on topic.*

Khalil was the topic. And narrating all her bloody imaginings to him wouldn't inspire any sort of confidence that she could help him. "I can't believe that with this level of aversion you left the situation to chance. You're too domineering and controlling to leave this up to fate. You fit the alpha-male mold even without the royalty stuff added on, but without even knowing me you counted on me chickening out. That's dumb. Maybe you should try to sleep more."

Antagonizing him probably wouldn't inspire confidence in her, either.

He looked sideways at her, his eyes off the road long enough to increase her worry. She took a deep breath and tried to relax her arms and shoulders. With the road rushing at her, she couldn't even release a fraction of that tension. She closed her eyes and tried again, channeling the physical manifestation of her fear to her right hand, where she could at least grip and abuse the armrest on the door and he might not see.

"You should try to sleep now," he said, his voice remarkably level.

"Yeah, that won't happen. I tried to sleep all the way here. It didn't work at all."

"Try again." Whatever anger she'd roused in him earlier was now gone. He could've been telling her the time of day for all the emotion reflected in his tone. Maybe she hadn't antagonized him so much after all. "We have a few hours' drive ahead of us."

"That may be, but..." But. But how much should she reveal? Would it make him act like less of a jerk if he knew what she was putting herself through for him? Or, more accurately, for Jamison? Or would he just use it as ammunition to get her back out of the truck and his presence? "I can't sleep in a moving car. Or plane. You should be able to understand someone not being able to sleep when they want to. I would love to go to sleep and block all this out, but I can't."

"The truck scares you?"

"All vehicles scare me," she muttered, and laid her head back, eyes still closed and arms now folded. "They're dangerous. People die all the time in car accidents."

Her voice became small and thready with the

last statement, reminding him of her history in a way that left him feeling unaccountably exposed and irritated. When their parents had died, Jamison had been away at school with him, and Khalil had witnessed firsthand how destructive it could be to lose both your parents in your formative years. He'd pulled Jamison back from his more destructive actions, distracting him in whatever way he'd been able to…including a couple of fistfights just because picking a fight and making Jay mad at him had been the better alternative to the things he'd been about to do.

Had anyone helped her with her grief? If she really was scared of all vehicles, she must have felt put through the wringer to get here.

And that thought didn't help, either. He wanted her to go, but using a fear born of the death of her parents to make her do what he wanted seemed like the worst kind of evil.

# CHAPTER THREE

ADALYN WHITE-KNUCKLED HER way through the desert trek. Now and then Khalil talked to her, and she knew it for what it was—distraction. However much he didn't want her there, when it mattered he was kind.

When they reached the camp location he turned and looked at her. "Take a few minutes to collect yourself before you get out, but don't take too long—the sun is reaching its zenith and the heat will rise very quickly now that the air-conditioning isn't running." Nevermind the now somewhat larger hole in the back window…

She nodded, finally letting herself look out the dusty windows at the little tent village. "Khalil?"

Saying his name stopped him from climbing down, though the door was open. He closed it enough to dampen their voices and kept his low. "Don't call me Khalil. I'm Zain while we're here.

The people know me by one name—having you use another will confuse things."

"Right." She nodded, still not thinking all that clearly. "Zain? There's a man running toward the truck."

That effectively took his attention from her. Zain-not-Khalil climbed down immediately and closed the door. Through the broken window she could hear them speaking, but that didn't mean she understood the words. What she did pick up on was the urgency in the man's voice. She leaned over to get a better view of him gesturing quickly toward one of the nearby tents.

"Adalyn, I need your help." Zain still sounded as authoritarian as Khalil had, but it made her move despite the earlier order to stay until she'd collected herself.

Adalyn climbed out and rounded the truck, meeting him at the back. "What's wrong?"

"His son is sick, and they've not been able to even keep water in him for two days."

Adalyn looked at the man and then at Khalil, nodding. "What do you want me to do?"

He'd already pulled open the back doors of the

truck and climbed in. "I want you to assist me. My medics aren't here yet, they went back to get your bag. So you're my nurse for now." In the back, he dug into a couple of different trunks and one cooler, pulling out supplies and stuffing them into an actual old-time doctor's bag.

"Nurse. Okay." She nodded, even if she wasn't sure what he wanted. "My clinical skills are rusty. I haven't actually treated injuries and illness since residency." Wait, what had he said? "Did you say that they went to get my bag?"

"Yes." He answered her question first, then added, "If you can follow instructions, you'll be fine."

"I can follow instructions." That probably wasn't the correct word for it, considering he was more giving orders than helpful instructions. But she could follow orders, too, when it suited her to do so.

"Get the doors. Then catch up." He jumped down, ushering the worried father with him off in the direction of the nearby camp.

Adalyn climbed into the truck, closed the trunks and flipped latches, then jumped down and did the same with the double doors at the back. Without the prospect of the vehicle moving, it lost its ability to scare her. Just having the chance to move and focus on something aside from imminent death let her compose herself. By the time she rounded the truck Khalil had reached a tent and she barely caught sight of him ducking to enter through the flap. Five more seconds and she might not have even known which tent he'd gone to.

As she hurried across the sandy expanse, the sun heated her dark hair to temperatures it never saw outside styling appliances. The long, thick, chestnut fall of hair carried that heat down her back so that by the time she reached the tent and called a greeting, she wished she'd pulled it up. Or cut it. Or maybe that she'd just let him head off into the desert on his own, rather than fighting to come with him. The man hadn't been wrong in warning her that she wasn't built for this kind of adventure. New Orleans heat was a different creature entirely.

"Zain?" She said his fake name, not knowing what the protocol was to enter someone's tent. You couldn't exactly knock or ring the bell.

"Come." He had that autocratic edge to his voice again.

She pulled open the flap and stepped inside. It smelled like a sick ward, but it was somewhat cooler than the air outside, something she was thankful for.

In the center of the tent a woman covered in layers of undoubtedly uncomfortable cloth held a small child in her lap. From the sweat matting his short hair and the color of his face, Adalyn could tell his fever had reached worrisome levels. Without asking any other questions, she stepped over and knelt with Khalil.

"Rotavirus," he said. "I need to set up an IV and get some fluids into him."

Khalil hadn't had much time to diagnose or examine before she'd gotten there, and that meant no time to sort out his supplies. When she opened the satchel and pulled out a bag of saline, she looked at him. "You expected rotavirus?"

"They had an outbreak of it a few weeks ago, and that's actually the vaccines I'd intended to give."

Rotavirus… What did she remember about

this? Not usually deadly, but it could be. Poor drinking water and sanitation usually caused outbreaks.

"Are any other children ill?" While she quietly asked for updates—just making sure that her rusty information wasn't going to cause tetanus—she fished out other supplies. The IV kit. Alcohol preps. Tourniquet.

"Not right now. But we're not going to be able to give the vaccine to him for a couple of days, just to make sure." The more he talked, the longer he was within the small tent, the more like a regular man he seemed…and less like an angry dictator. "They should be healthy before it's given."

Though he looked somewhat severe still, tension no longer stood out in cords down his neck. No matter what kind of edge he had in his voice when he spoke to her, when he spoke to these people…his people…Khalil's voice became much gentler. She didn't even need to understand the words to know what he was doing. Comforting. Reassuring. Explaining treatment.

The things a good doctor did. Was this the man that Jamison called his best friend?

Adalyn waited for a lull in the conversation to ask, "How can we keep the other children from getting it?"

"My medics have a new purification system they'll set up when they get here. And we'll see what we can do for other interventions." He looked at her, his honey-brown eyes taking on the quality of examination, and before he even said anything she knew what he was looking at. Inside the tent, sheltered from the sun, her skin still burned. She was going pink. Her sunburn had already started. And she'd probably have freckles before they got back to the palace.

"I didn't swim in sunblock before I left this morning, which I should have done. I will remedy that when they get here with my bag." It still shocked her that he'd given in on that. She kind of wished she'd been nicer to him in the truck, and she hadn't thanked him yet... "I misunderstood. When you said 'Fine,' I thought you just meant you weren't going to quarrel with me, but you meant the bag, right?"

He nodded and tied the band around the unconscious boy's arm, then began prodding for a vein.

"Thank you…Doctor." She'd almost called him Khalil, it had been on the tip of her tongue. She should probably stop thinking of him as Khalil if she wanted to maintain his cover. Which she did. He'd done something kind for her in getting her bag, maybe she could turn this situation around and still get him to let her help him. Maybe tomorrow after he'd had a night of sleep he'd be more reasonable about it. Maybe she could win him over, get his cooperation…and shorten the length of time she'd need to stay there, away from home.

Despite feeling and feeling for a vein, he still hadn't picked up the needle or alcohol prep.

"It's hard to find a vein when they're very dehydrated," Adalyn said. This was actually something she was good at.

"I know."

"Of course you do. I'm sorry. I didn't mean to insinuate you didn't. I was thinking out loud. But, as rusty as most of my clinical skills are, I'm actually really good at IVs." He looked at her, the weight of his gaze settling on her, considering. He'd let her do it if she convinced him. "I can hit it. If you like. It's actually something that I do regularly for an elderly neighbor. She's not a child, but she's got tiny veins."

"Your neighbor needs you to set up an IV for her?"

"I do blood draws for her weekly to take with her to her anticoagulation appointment. I draw in the morning when I get in from work, we put it into a thermos and she takes it with her. They can never hit the vein without several stabs, so she prefers it if I do it." Rather than give a fuller recitation of her most recent IVs, she figured she'd said enough for him to decide and quieted to let him work it out.

"I appreciate the offer."

The woman who held her child hadn't said anything, and Adalyn didn't know how much English she understood, if any. So she did what she could and smiled, reaching over to pat the woman's arm. "It'll be okay. We're going to help him." And then asked Khalil, "What's his name?"

"I don't know," he answered, but ignored her offer in favor of palpating the tiny arm for a vein.

"Upper arm might be better. I'd say leg, but they can kick those out pretty easy."

He flipped off the tourniquet and moved to the boy's other arm, starting over again.

Her keys…

Adalyn patted the many pockets on her pants, unsnapped a thigh pocket and fished out the set, then snatched the little laser she played with her neighbor's cat with.

"What are you doing?"

"This will help." She pressed the button to turn on the cheap little laser pointer and pressed it to the boy's arm where he was palpating for a vein. Through the thin layer of baby fat the light illuminated the dark pathways that were blood vessels. "That help?"

"What the…?" He blinked and let her track the light over the boy's skin. There were special infrared lights he'd heard of for illuminating veins, but he'd never seen such a cheap-looking gadget do it. "Is that infrared?"

"Wee sight illuminators are best, and I have one

for Mrs. Stiverson's sticks, but I didn't bring it with me. I've used this in a pinch before, though. I probably should have left my keys at the p—" She stopped herself before *palace* came out of her mouth. "At home." A slightly flummoxed shake of her head and she moved past it. "But I'm kind of afraid something will happen and I'll be separated from something important if I don't have it with me at all times."

If he kicked her out of the country, she meant. Khalil could read between those lines easily enough.

The thought had occurred to him.

Rather than comment, he reached for another alcohol prep, swabbed the skin and then lifted her hand to swab the tip of the light and the area she'd pressed against the small boy's arm. When he was certain that it was all disinfected and the skin illuminated, he felt right over one of the larger, dark vessels. "It's not all that deep," he murmured, getting a nod from her.

"And there's a small amount of thickness on the edges, probably the walls of the vessel, but if you aim for the center you'll be fine."

After a few more words of reassurance for the mother, he asked the boy's name and gave instructions on holding him snugly in case he woke up and began to struggle.

"His name is Nadim, and he's three," Khalil said in quiet English, since Adalyn had wanted to know. "If he wakes up, drop the light and hold his legs. She'll have his top half, but if he has use of his legs he'll be able to put up more of a fight."

"Of course." She kept the light against the boy's skin, but with her other hand reached down and wrapped her fingers around the tiny ankle closest to Khalil.

So, she could follow orders.

Carefully, he threaded the line into the boy's vein and when rewarded with a blood return attached a saline flush to double-check. Sometime in all this she'd dropped the light and had taken over holding the line so it didn't slip out.

When he'd confirmed that the vein was indeed intact still, he taped down the cannula and she hooked the tubing up to the bag and stood, letting gravity feed the fluid down to the end before he attached it to the needle.

"How are we going to hang it?" she asked.

"We'll have a stand when the medics get here."

"I made them late."

"No. Well, yes, but you're earning your keep." Her little cheap key chain light had saved him a lot of headache. Khalil might not want her there to help him, but he could appreciate the help she provided for the people in his care. "I might not have hit that vein without your trick, and most assuredly would not have on the first try. Where'd you learn that?"

"It's something I always check on pretty much every light I get my hands on." She smiled at him, her first honest, unguarded smile. Her cheeks bunched, bringing the pink closer to her green eyes so that they seemed all the greener, and gave that suggestion again of innocence. Beneath her aggravation at him there was a sweetness about her.

"My dad and I used to put flashlights to our cheeks, noses, whatever…then turn off the lights and make faces at one another with glowing cheeks and black hollow-looking eyes. Got me in the habit of checking different lights against my skin."

He spoke again with the mother, giving her instructions and explaining what he was going to do. When he stopped speaking and looked at her again, Adalyn continued her story. "I had to give a presentation in college and got my own pointer because I wanted to be the best. I was nervous talking in front of everyone, but I managed to get through the whole thing by distracting myself by pressing it against my arm or hand and watching the veins get illuminated. Coping mechanism that turned into a trick that helped me in residency. I was all about tricks that might make me better able to do the job. I'm not a natural, like Jamison."

"That why you went into sleep medicine?"

"No." She turned off the light and stashed it in her pocket again, then began cleaning up the garbage left behind from the containers.

Clearly she wasn't going to give him more information than that. Not unless he dragged it out of her.

For the time being he hung the bag on a bit of

wood at the top of the tent, and when it didn't cause the thing to bow or collapse, he turned his attention back to Adalyn. "Why did you pick sleep medicine?"

"Because it was a good fit for me. I understand sleep problems."

"Are you an insomniac?"

"No." She stuffed the trash into one of the bigger bags and then set it beside his, where it would be easy to dispose of. When her task was finished she rubbed the boy's leg in a way that comforted the mother, who was clearly so worried that she didn't even have anything to ask or talk about. Her attention entirely focused on her son and the line now feeding life-giving fluids into him that he couldn't vomit back up, but she seemed reassured simply by their presence.

Adalyn might be rusty, but she did have the touch.

"I had nightmares when my parents died." Her words came so softly he could have missed them if he'd not been looking at her. "It took me a long time to learn how to manage them. I think that's why I find sleep so interesting. Everyone shrugs off the importance of rest, but it's fascinating how much the body does while you're sleeping. And that's not even counting what the mind gets up to in dreams..."

Bad things, that's what his mind got up to in dreams.

Maybe she would understand if he just told her the basics. That he had nightmares and his insomnia was more of a choice than a symptom.

Not that he wanted to even go that far with his explanations. She'd want to know why he had nightmares—it didn't take a mental leap to give significance to the lack of sleep as being preferable to the nightmares. And dreams that bad... she'd want to know details. What were they about? What did they make him feel? Things he just couldn't bring himself to talk about. He didn't even like to think about them.

"Jay never mentioned that about you." Or maybe he had and Khalil hadn't been paying sufficient attention when they'd spoken on the phone. He certainly hadn't been able to come up with a reason not to keep her from coming—at least one that Jay would buy. He hadn't bought the one about the country having recently been in a civil war, and that had seemed like a given.

"I never really let Jamison know how bad they were, so please don't tell him." She shrugged, but not a hint of the earlier smile remained, even in her eyes. "I didn't let anyone but my therapist know. My aunt and uncle sent me to therapy to deal with the deaths, so I talked to her about it all. And we worked on it together."

"She was a sleep specialist?"

"No. Not in any way, but she understood enough to get us started, and she dug into any studies she could find as well, learned all she could to help me."

Voices outside the tent alerted him. "They're here." He looked down at the woman and her son and crouched back down. He made a quick introduction between Adalyn and the mother—since he'd neglected it before—and repeated the instructions he'd given earlier.

Afterward he turned to Adalyn and went through the list with her again in English and in more detail.

"You're leaving me here?"

"I'm going to help them set up the tents, and I'll send someone in with the stand for the IV. Be careful when you transfer it from where I've got it standing. The last thing they need is for the tent to collapse on them while they're trying to get the little guy well."

"What if she says something to me? I don't understand…" He could tell she was trying to keep the alarm out of her voice, but the way she turned to keep her face hidden from the mother but remained entirely visible to him let him know.

Was there anything the woman wasn't scared of?

Travel.

Cars.

Planes.

Letting her brother down.

Being alone with a woman she couldn't understand.

Unclean drinking water. Actually, he couldn't blame her for that one. But, really, how had she managed the backbone required to launch that rock at his truck?

"I'm not going far, Adalyn. I'll have them bring

you a walkie-talkie, too. If you need anything, just call me on it and I'll come. You need to stay out of the sun—you've already begun to burn, and that will no doubt feel worse when the sun goes down. Setting up means a lot of heavy labor and today we're doing the tents and setting up the purification system for the water. It would be better if you stayed inside."

Somewhere in his list of reasons she'd started to look less alarmed and worried. Either that or she was getting control of her eyebrows, since they were in more or less a neutral position now. "Just make sure that they get the walkie-talkies and the stand in here quickly."

He nodded and she turned back to the woman, rubbing her arm through the layers of fabric.

"Remember who you are calling on the radio." He tried to give her the kind of reminder that wouldn't give away his charade, and would make sure she didn't give it away, either. He hoped. Zain. Not Khalil.

She nodded and murmured, "I'll remember, Dr. Zain." A small comfort at least. Maybe she'd even remember it if she had to call him in an emergency situation.

He headed out and, after he relayed the orders for what she needed to one of his men, grabbed a walkie-talkie and strapped it to his belt, then went to help unload the trucks.

Even with the heat and the heavy labor, Khalil didn't mind helping set up. It was such a different situation than at the palace that it calmed him. Routine, blending in with everyone else. Anonymity wasn't something he'd ever really had— even when he'd been away in England at school, people had known who he was. They were just less likely to be cowed by it than those in his home country. But before coming to Merirach, when he and Jay had gone on medical missions into other countries—places where no one had known or cared who he was or what he did—it had been heaven.

As they pounded long rods deep into the ground and started pitching the tent, some of the village men came over to help them get it lifted.

They started quietly, but as they worked their

normal comraderie came swinging into full force and soon one of the young men had asked about Adalyn. Dark hair. Pale skin. Green eyes. Of course she'd attracted attention. But beyond the coloring that gave her an exotic edge, she had something else that took her from pretty to the kind of looks that'd hang in any man's mind. It couldn't be the innocent way she had, and it really couldn't be how many things frightened her, though that did somewhat rouse a protective instinct in him. It was something else.

But how could he explain who she was?

If he said she was there to treat him, they'd think he wasn't capable of being a good doctor to them.

If he said she was just a colleague, then at least a couple of the young men would think about her in a way that made him instantly tense. Jamison wouldn't want her having a surprise desert marriage, no matter what goods she got in exchange for her hand.

Khalil wouldn't like it, either.

Even Zain wouldn't like it.

He had to say something…

"She's my mistress." He said the only thing he could think of, with the hot sun beating down on him and the hours of not sleeping behind him.

For the first few seconds after the words had come out a kind of ominous quality lingered around them and he couldn't put his finger on why, but his inner caveman woke up again, entirely too pleased with this lie.

He felt his pulse increase, but before he got the pole he'd been working on placed a riot of laughter broke out among the men. They all had their ideas about American women, and that just confirmed the worst of it.

They might not entirely condone it but, as his mistress, she'd sleep in his tent and none of the men would question it. He hadn't thought about where she'd sleep before, but that certainly had to be what would need to happen. As his colleague, there wouldn't be any sort of ownership. She might still be up for grabs, but if he claimed her as his own in some fashion, they'd respect that boundary. They respected him, so no matter what they thought about her morals she'd be protected.

The more he thought about it the better he liked the idea.

Actually, it might work out even better than that. She didn't even like him seeing her knees, so how would she feel about being thought of as his mistress? Would that be enough to convince her to let him call the chopper and send her home? If he had learned one thing about Adalyn, it was that she didn't like surprises. Well, she didn't like much of anything—except maybe illuminating her skin with different lights and talking about sleep—but surprises were probably right at the top of her list of things she didn't like. Right there with motor vehicles.

# CHAPTER FOUR

THIS WAS NOT exactly how Adalyn had expected the trip to go.

Granted, she hadn't had that much time to contemplate what she was getting herself into. Last night all she'd really been able to think had been *sleep*. Then this morning and in the truck she'd been too preoccupied with everything else to wrap her mind around what the little tent village was going to be like.

She couldn't liken the situation to anything she'd experienced. The only quasi-normal part was watching Nadim sleep, as well as the other medical aspects returning to her. She'd focus on those things. That would make everything seem less foreign and scary.

When Nadim woke, she got him to drink some liquid antinausea medicine. When that stayed down, she got a little fever-reducing medicine into him, too. Khalil had… No. She had to call him Zain, think of him as Zain. Back in the palace she probably had to call him by a title, so maybe the only place to call him Khalil was when sleep was near.

Zain might want a report on treatment, but she went into his satchel for the stethoscope instead and listened to little Nadim's belly first.

Zain hadn't told her to call with any good news, only emergencies, but a quick look at the IV they'd been giving him confirmed that they'd be in need before much longer. He'd taken nearly the whole bag already and still hadn't needed to relieve himself. Not that she could ask, but he didn't seem as if he needed to.

Right. She needed her translating dictionary. She should also get that other bag and hang it, though perhaps on a lower titration rate.

"I need to get more." She said the words in English because she just didn't have the words to communicate properly.

Her words had two sets of dark eyes looking at her. Adalyn stood and pointed to the bag, and with a series of gestures led the mother through the fluids situation. Almost out, easy to see in the bag. She pointed to herself and then out and held up two fingers…

When the poor haggard mother nodded Adalyn returned the nod and grabbed Khalil's satchel to trot back out.

The sun still beat down on her, baking her head and back, but the sooner she got back to the trucks the sooner she'd be saved from the blistering sun.

Near the truck, two tents had been erected, but none of the men were within sight now. Maybe they'd moved on to the water system.

Once in the truck, she located the saline quickly, then dug her dictionary from her bag and grabbed a few other supplies they'd need.

Her walkie-talkie crackled and she heard Khalil—Zain—through it.

"Where are you?"

Right. Of course he'd come back as soon as she'd stepped out, so he'd think she'd abandoned them.

Grabbing it off her belt, she pressed the button and spoke back. "The fluids were running out and he hasn't had to… No urine output so far or indication that he needs to go. I came out to the truck to get another bag and see if you had a cooling blanket, which you do, so I'm taking that to them, too. He kept down the antiemetic and fever reducer, but his fever is still higher than I'd like it to be."

"You should have called."

"It wasn't an emergency."

"You're my responsibility while we're out here, Adalyn. You could get hurt wandering about by yourself."

She could get hurt?

That's why she should have called? "You didn't say that before. You said emergency. But I will let you know before I go to the truck again. Anything else?"

"Come back." There it was again, the irritated tone that had dominated everything he'd said to her when not conversing in front of their patient.

As if it had even needed to be said. What kind of idiot would she have to be to stay outside and bake in the sun or the back of this darned truck—which might actually be hot enough to fire bricks?

"Ten-four," she muttered, because that's what people said in the movies when they used these things, and using the slang felt just bratty enough to make her feel a tiny bit better about her situation.

Which was worse? Dealing with the man who swung back and forth between acceptance and annoyance, or dealing with the entirely unfamiliar and therefore unsafe surroundings? She should be the one having mood swings, because she couldn't judge from one second to the next what his mood would be. If she'd had to guess earlier, she'd have said that her going out to get the fluids and supplies to take care of his patient would have made him happy. And she'd have been wrong.

With her supplies gathered up, and a couple of bottles of water from the cooler added to her loot, she headed back out of the truck, which she'd found imminently more pleasant without the motor running, even with the heat.

Maybe she could sleep in the thing later when night came and everything cooled off. There probably wouldn't be any stinging or biting critters in the safe confines of the truck.

By the time she got back her shirt was plastered to her back, and she'd developed a thirst so keen she could've downed both bottles of water.

Kha— Zain looked at her with a sharpness that confirmed his pendulum as being firmly on the annoyance side of the Sahara right now. "Here." She handed him the bag of fluid and then crouched down beside Nadim and his mother to shake out the cooling blanket. The look of alarm blasted at her from the mother made her pause. Zain offered her no assistance, not explaining what the blanket was, just looking on. Adalyn did the only thing she could—laid the material against the bare skin of the mother's hand to let her feel the difference between this and a regular blanket.

When she smiled, Adalyn took it as consent and laid the material on the boy's chest then tucked it around his legs. He opened his eyes and looked at the strange material with wonder, then pulled it up to his cheek and smiled over the edge at Adalyn. If nothing else, he was more comfortable.

"I forgot we had that," Zain murmured, after

changing the fluid bag and sitting beside her again. "You look about ready to fall over."

"I thought that our heat would be comparable. Guess I was wrong. The sun just feels so hot. I should have tied my hair back. I didn't even bring any hair ties."

"We could use the tourniquet."

"Maybe later. I'm not so far gone right now that I'd like my hair ripped to shreds by uncovered rubber."

He took one of the bottles and drank deeply from it, prompting her to do the same thing. Hydration was even more important when they were probably going to use all of the saline in their inventory to take care of little Nadim.

When he'd drained the whole bottle he capped it and asked the mother something. Soon she was laying the boy on the mat and tucking the cooling blanket back around him. With a quick trip to the side of the tent, she came back with a comb and a piece of thick ribbon.

"She's going to braid your hair for you," Zain said.

Adalyn looked up at him. "Why? Do I look that bad?"

"You look hot and miserable, but keep in mind that she understands how hot it can be where the sun hits black." He went to check the filtration of Nadim's IV, then sat beside the kid, who was now actually awake enough to look miserable.

Adalyn opened her mouth to say something, but the soft cadence of Zain's speech to the boy stopped her. He spoke gently. Not understanding a word, she could only guess from the way the conversation remained one-sided and the way Nadim watched Zain with interest that he was telling the boy a story. Another glimpse of the kind of man she could see her brother being friends with?

When Nadim's mom pulled a short stool behind her and gestured, Adalyn sat down and pulled her hair free of her collar to flop down her back in a heavy thump, helping as much as she could.

Soon the comb was sliding through her hair, working through the tangles. It all happened very quickly. One moment her hair was baking her and the next it had been braided at the neck and coiled into what she could only assume was a bun, though how the woman managed to secure it with only the ribbon, she couldn't say.

"Thank you." She said it in English, then re-membered how to say it properly to her in a tongue she would understand, and repeated the words.

Zain said something else to her and gestured to the boy. "She's going to get their supper started, and I told her we'd stay with him while she cooked."

By the time the tents were set up the afternoon had turned to evening. With the sun low on the horizon, Adalyn was no longer quite so hot, but then again getting her hair off her back had gone a long way toward lowering her body temperature.

Nadim had taken the whole of the second bag of fluid before needing to relieve himself. He was on the mend, or at least helped as sufficiently as they could do in the desert. There wasn't any cure for rotavirus—and while it wasn't usually fatal, it could be. Especially in this climate where proper hydration was a daily battle even when someone wasn't vomiting and worse.

Zain herded Adalyn from the small tent to one of those the men had erected that afternoon. He said very little, at least very little she understood. He must have bought a truckload of the walkie-talkies, because the family was given one to call for help in the night, though it didn't look as if they'd need it.

"One of us should set an alarm and check in on them during the night," Adalyn said.

With the sun low on the horizon, the temperature was dropping, but the large white tents looked like heaven from the outside.

"Someone will."

She would have gone into the first tent, but his hand landed at the small of her back to steer her past it to the second.

Once they stepped into the white tent she felt immediately cooler. Just not cool enough to keep standing up. The short nap the night before had pretty much only been enough to keep her on her feet, and the weariness she felt screamed for her to sit and conserve energy at every opportunity. She scanned the tent for the optimal place to sit down, one that would allow her to remain awake a little longer.

There were bedrolls on the ground, a lantern and a simple rug that spanned the vast majority of the floor of the moderately sized domicile, but it was all terribly ordinary.

"This is where you sleep?"

"This is where we sleep." He stepped past her and folded himself down onto one of the bedrolls, his legs pitching up at lazy angles so that he could lean his forearms on them. And the look on his face… She couldn't identify it. She'd have said smug if those hooded eyes didn't also travel down her body and then back up again…

Adalyn had sometimes been on the receiving end of almost tangible looks before—usually during high school when baleful looks from popular classmates had sometimes felt as real as a slap in the face. She'd just never have guessed a simple look could feel like a caress, but her skin prickled with awareness.

It took effort to think, let alone speak. She had to get this under control.

"Just us two here? What about the…medics?"

Whom she'd only so far seen at a distance, and who looked like anything but medics. "Or are they really security?"

"Hakem and Suhail are both trained as security, but Hakem is also trained as a paramedic. Good eye. What gave them away?" His intimate look faded, though his eyes still showed an interest she couldn't begin to wrap her mind around.

"They both look like they could bench-press a car." She folded herself down onto her bedroll opposite to him, but then spotted her bag and crawled to it to open it and dig out a protein bar. Distraction. Plus, she hadn't eaten anything all day and had no taste for the adventure that would be required to eat whatever food these strangers gave her. Sustenance was a necessity. She tore one open and settled back on her roll.

"They sleep in the other tent."

She glanced around the tent and back to the bar while working on the wrapper. She'd come up with a plan during the hours with Nadim, and it was the only idea she had on how to salvage this situation.

Win Khalil over so he'd let her help him. Good plan.

Think of him the way she thought of Jamison. Treat him the way she treated her brother.

"We should sleep in Khalil's tent." She said his name quietly but kept on with her plan. Teasing and joking around. That's what she usually did with Jamison. "I bet it's fancy. And golden. With air-conditioning. And maybe a pool. Too bad we have to stay in Zain's tent." Would he get that she was teasing him? Any friend of her brother would need a good sense of humor. "I thought that other tent was the clinic."

"It is," he said, only confirming that he'd heard her going on about Khalil's tent with the tilt of one corner of his mouth… Half a smile was all that had got her. "We don't leave it empty once it's got supplies inside. The vaccines, needles, gloves and alcohol are not irreplaceable, but I don't want anyone coming to harm because they tried to use something without knowing the proper way."

Khalil's eyes were still fixed on her—and more specifically on her protein bar—in a way that made her feel nervous, but for once it didn't seem as if they were about to quarrel. "Did I do something wrong?"

"You brought food?"

Or maybe they were about to quarrel.

"I..." She looked at the thing she'd planned on eating in privacy somewhere that would minimize the amount of offense not wanting to eat their food could cause. "I packed them and water tablets because, you know, you hear horror stories about people eating something lovely in a foreign place and then getting terrible gastrointestinal distress or some other illness. I just wanted safe food." And before he could say anything else, or before she said something wrong, she crammed one end of the sawdust-flavored gritty protein bar into her mouth and broke off a chunk.

Attempting to chew the thing required water, and if she didn't get some fast, it might suck half the moisture out of her body.

"Good, is it?"

She looked back at him, grinning around the mouthful as she chewed and chewed and chewed…one finger up to signal to him that she would speak when her mouth was not full of wood chips and fake chocolate.

"I bet we could build something out of those. A barbecue pit maybe," he said. So he did have a sense of humor.

If she laughed now, she'd definitely choke to death. Just a little longer, and maybe one bite would be enough for her. Once it was clear, her jaw burned from the effort and she was seriously reconsidering having another bite. "I guess I wasn't shopping for flavor."

"Just safety from villainous foreign foods."

She sighed, nodded, and he leaned behind him to grab a water bottle to pass to her. She took it and drank eagerly. Foreign villainous water… "Thank you."

"It was either that or watch you turn into a pru—"

The loud sounds of her swallowing drowned out the last of what he'd said. But somehow… "Did you just call me a prude?"

"Is that what it sounded like?"

"Yes." And something she'd heard before, back

in the days when she'd actually cared enough to try to fit in with other people. When she'd had aggressive and hurtful words lobbed at her regularly. Fat. Prone to hysterics. Nerd. Prude… "I'm not a prude. I just don't…"

Khalil watched her cheeks go pink to the point that the rosy hue surpassed the mild sunburn she'd gotten on her window-side arm during their drive and the bridge of her nose and apples of her cheeks from her short trips through the camp earlier.

He kind of wished he had called her a prude now. "I said prune. You know, a plum that has dried out? From that sawdust brick drying you out."

Even her ears had turned red. She looked at him long and hard, as if he was going to lie about that.

"Well, I'm not. I'm neither."

"Good. That is actually good. Because I need to speak to you about something." It may have been an accident, but it was an opening, and he'd take whatever opening he could get. "The village men were asking about you. Who you were. I've never brought a woman with me before."

She folded the top of the bar's package closed and carefully laid it beside her, the kind of slow meticulous actions that screamed wariness. "What did you tell them?"

"I told them you were my mistress."

He delivered the news matter-of-factly and waited for her reaction. If the label didn't distress her, he'd have to look for another weapon. Her reaction would have to inform the next move.

It took a couple of seconds for the words to register, and he knew as soon as they had. Her mouth fell open and she looked toward the exit and back, confirming the power of the attack.

"Why did you do that?"

Khalil let his gaze do the wandering again. He'd been fighting to control his desire to look at her since their meeting in her room the previous night. The image of her in her underthings had burned into his mind and helped inform him now as he took in supple limbs, the light freckling of her normally pale skin, the way the white cotton top clung to her from the heat and the sweat moistening her skin. He remembered what white cotton looked like against her flesh.

"Khalil?" She whispered his name, the heat having found a way into her voice, as well.

She'd asked him why. Right.

"Because we're sharing a tent, and when they asked about you it was with lust in their eyes." Lust he could understand.

Adalyn looked at the door again but seemed to shrink into the bedroll. "How did that mistress thing help? Now they're going to think that I'm a...I'm... That I'm..."

"That you're mine." He filled in, "It was either mistress or wife. You were the one determined to come with me."

She fidgeted with the top of her water bottle, unscrewing and screwing the cap over and over. "Then you should have said wife. At least then they wouldn't think I was a woman of...low morals. I know that in this part of the world that sort of thing really matters." She tightened the cap and dropped the bottle beside her. "I'm trying to help you, and you're making it hard again."

"Am I?" Hands on the rug, he leveraged himself over to sit beside her on her bedroll, the desire to stretch her out and pretend she really was his nearly overwhelming all reason.

But there was always that wariness about her.

"What is it costing you if some people you will never see again think that you and I will be naked in here together later?"

"I'll be embarrassed," she whispered, but a blush continued down her neck and over the small patch of exposed skin on her chest. Embarrassed she might be, but the idea excited her, too. "And I won't be able to understand what they say about me. They'll say harsh things. Or they'll laugh and clap you on the back maybe. Way to go, Zain! You got yourself a travel-sized floozy to keep you warm on those chilly desert nights."

He could still make this work. It might even be better if it excited her. Then she could leave on friendly terms with him. Just not as friendly as they'd both like. The forbidden quality could work in his favor. They must think of Jamison after all. And if they couldn't control themselves, she'd have to go... "And you like that idea." He leaned in just enough to feel the heat pouring off her.

"No, I don't! I don't...I haven't dated much... I have..." She couldn't even bring herself to say the words. Either that or she was flustered enough by the fact that he was coming on to her that she didn't know what to think.

"Have past lovers complained, Adalyn?" Knock her off-kilter, then make a move...

# CHAPTER FIVE

"THAT IS NONE of your business!"

Her voice pitched up into a higher register, enough to cause Suhail—cooking outside—to call to him for a security check. He shouted back that everything was fine and cupped a hand over her mouth, and an ache formed in the center of his palm where her plump lower lip brushed his skin, hot and moist…soft. "Don't scream. It will alarm everyone."

She jerked her head back, lowering her voice to an angry whisper. "I don't need to explain my sexual history to you. I am here as your doctor. And this is very inappropriate behavior. You should sit on your pallet. Not here with me. And not… You know what? You're right. It is nothing to me what these people think of me. I'm just an American trollop. I'm sure that they'd have thought that regardless. But don't think for a second that I'm going to…"

The angrier she got, the pinker she got, the more heated her whispers. And despite the tirade, with his close proximity, she kept looking at his mouth as she made her displeasure known. When she looked at his mouth, subconsciously she'd lick her lips or for a fraction of a second lose her train of thought.

He wanted it to. His train of thought hadn't gone this far when he'd been plotting earlier. For once he'd had no idea how she'd respond to a kiss. Would it scare her off? Make her agree to go back to the palace and then home? Make her want more?

What reaction did he even want? For her to kiss him back or run for the hills? Theoretically, and for entirely different reasons, either reaction would do. Only, now he wasn't all that certain he could follow through on the idea to kiss her senseless and send her away for the sake of his friendship with her brother.

All the planning didn't give him what he needed. Curling his hand around that bun her hair had been worked into, he dragged her to meet him and caught her with her mouth open. That plump little lip that had tormented his palm, that he'd watched her repeatedly dampen with her tongue, he caught it with his lips. A tiny sound of surprise and alarm sounded in her throat, but it took very little for her to relax into his grip. Her head fell back and it took no coaxing at all for him to gain entrance into her mouth.

Suddenly, it was no longer about scaring her away. It was about the feeling that rolled over him as his hand left her hair and he wrapped his arms around her. He'd wanted to taste her since that first night when he'd caught her in her underwear, the first time she'd blushed for him. It was pure. It might be pure lust, but she wouldn't let him kiss her if she saw him as a monster or a villain.

Small hands fisted the material of his shirt as if she wanted to tear it off him but could only manage to twist and tug, helpless in the face of unexpected need that might ruin them.

Her kisses went from timid and accepting to wanting to ravenous in the space of heartbeats.

Despite the heat, she still smelled sweet. He pressed her back into the blanket, rolling with her until he could feel more of her soft body against his.

He could forget like this. Forget everything—the world, his responsibilities—just revel in what she could give him. Wrap her around every painful part of him.

Except it was a lie. One he wanted more than anything to be real in that moment.

She wasn't really his. This was a cover story, maybe a dangerous game of chicken…but nothing more. She wasn't his, she was Jamison's sister.

He heard a manly throat clearing and reluctantly broke the kiss to look toward the tent flap.

Suhail stood there with two dinner bowls, and not even a hint of judgment on his face. Both men Khalil traveled with were loyal to the core and had been with him almost all the time since the coup, and Hakem longer. For years. Since before the coup. Through it. Khalil still didn't understand why Hakem stayed with him—and stayed loyal—after that…

They were the only ones now outside the Quinn family who knew what he got up to when he left the palace.

He nodded and Suhail put the bowls down at the foot of the bedrolls, and though he still held Adalyn in his arms, she'd grown tenser since those heady moments when she'd rolled pliantly back onto the bed with him.

He slid his arms from beneath her and sat up while his willpower remained.

"You kissed me," she whispered, slow blinks and speech sounding just the slightest bit drugged.

Not so hard to understand, though he'd rather put it down to sleep deprivation than some kind of real connection. "You kissed me back," he reminded her. Yes, he may have started it, but she'd participated as feverishly as he had. If Suhail hadn't come into the tent, could he have stopped himself?

Whatever the answer, Khalil didn't even have to question whether he could maintain that control when she was close enough to grab again.

He scooted back over to his bedroll. A quick

lean to the side and he grabbed the bowls and set one in front of her. "It's nothing fancy. Rice and some cooked meat. Eat it. It is better for you than that thing you were eating."

She looked at the bowl for a long moment, lightly brushing her lower lip with her fingertips as if she couldn't quite figure out what had just happened.

"Stop that," he muttered, looking at the food instead of her. If she kept stroking her lip that way, even unconsciously as she seemed to be doing, he was going to go right back to her bed and do things she'd—

"Stop what?"

"Touching your mouth. Just…eat."

She pulled her hand away and focused on the bowl. "How do you know it won't make me sick?"

"What's exotic about meat and rice? Nothing. I wouldn't give you food that would make you ill." He sat opposite her again on his own bed-roll, hungry enough to not wait for her.

"I'm not sure I believe you."

"You should believe me," he said. "What kind

of man purposefully makes his mistress ill? Not one who wants—"

She kicked him.

Not hard, but one of her feet popped out from her cross-legged position and bounced off his shin.

Yeah, he'd deserved a kick.

A soon as her foot had flown, she tucked it back under her knee and began eating what he'd given her.

Adalyn grabbed the bowl and took a bite. Any consequences were preferable to sitting there, savoring the taste of his kisses that still lingered on her lips.

As the first bite went down she had to admit the food—simple as it was—tasted good. Much better than those nutrient-dense monstrosities she'd been intent on eating, just not as good as he had.

Next time she traveled, which she hoped would be *never*, she'd have to have some kind of test phase where she actually tried to eat different kinds of bars until she found one moderately edible. And she'd make some kind of rule about kissing the countries' royalty, if she managed to stumble across them.

Stupid.

"Tell me something," Khalil said, breaking back into her thoughts even as she tried to banish him and the taste of him with the rice and meat.

Once more his gaze felt tangible, like a touch, as if he was still feeling hot and heavy over her. She kept staring at her dinner, not trusting herself to watch him putting food in his mouth.

Tell him something? Like...that no one ever kissed her like that before? That the few times she'd gone out on dates they had been an utter disappointment. None of the fireworks she'd read about in books. Not even a sparkler or a single match's worth of passion. But here, in this tent, with this man who infuriated her, her toes had curled and her back had arched from the current zipping down her spine and everywhere he'd touched her.

"Anything. Tell me what you're thinking."

"No." The word launched from her with the

same force she'd felt zinging through her at his touch. She took another bite to give herself time to think and slid back to the subject of him. His sleep problems. Though talking about sleep or thinking about sleep made her want to just go to sleep and try to work out what his angle was tomorrow, when she'd have a handful of functioning brain cells. Which would have to be after she'd filled her belly and fallen into the coma she planned to fall into. "Tell me about your sleep thing."

"Talking about you would be more interesting. You're a late bloomer."

"You mentioned that I didn't look like my picture. How old was I in the picture? It couldn't be all that recent because I've seen Jamison in person once in the past two years."

"When was that?"

"Last week." She sighed, shaking her head. "We were having bread pudding at my favorite restaurant when you called him. That is how I got wrangled into this." Yes. Talk about Jamison. Talk about how Khalil had caught them during the rare visit when Jamison could apply pres-

sure in person. It was easier to dodge promises and brotherly manipulation when you were
only speaking on the phone or in email, but in
person? He could be extremely annoying. And
persistent. And, if she made it back alive, she'd
be sure to tell Jamison it wasn't "good for her,"
as he'd said it would be about twenty million
times.

"I think you were in college," he said, bringing her focus back to the topic.

She looked up and caught him grinning, a lop-
sided smile that didn't look at all as if he was
making fun of her. "So, before medical school.
You saw the pudgy me."

"You were a bit rounder than you are now,"
he confirmed. "Not unattractive, just different."

"Medical school was hard, but the dietary
courses helped." She pushed past the subject
before he worked around to calling her a prude
again. Not that he had before—according to
him—but it surprised her how much that had
upset her. Not that the kissing hadn't made up for
it, but…that really wasn't the topic. She wasn't
here for kissing. This was not a vacation fling in

the Caribbean, no matter how nice those sounded in books. Two different kinds of sandy destinations. "I want to know why you sleep better in the tent."

"I told you…"

"No, you didn't. You just said that you have insomnia at the—"

"Don't say that word," he said, cutting her off before she said *palace* where anyone might accidentally overhear and understand.

"Sorry." She took the final bite of her rice dish, amazed she'd eaten it all, and set it aside. "Tell me what you think about when you're going to sleep."

"I don't know. What I have to do, I suppose." He definitely didn't want to talk about it. And that was too bad.

"When you're here that's what you think about?"

"Yes. When I'm on one of these medical missions I think about the people. The patients, and what they need… What I need to provide for them."

His words didn't really convey any emotion,

but there was a tension in his voice, a tenor of deception among the mundane words. "And that's different than when you're home?"

"I guess."

"You don't think about your other duties in the same way as you think about your medical duties?"

"Would you?"

"I don't know," Adalyn said, shrugging as she untied her shoes and slipped toward the head of the bedroll. The more she immersed herself in the riddle of his sleep issues, the easier it was to stop thinking about the way his mouth had seared hers. "I've never done anything but my medical duties, not since finishing my training." Because that didn't sound extremely lame. But she liked her quiet life. She liked the safety of it. Not like here, where at any second... "Hey, what will keep things from coming into the tent while we're asleep?"

"What things?"

"People. Critters that are poisonous. Snakes and spiders and scorpions."

Khalil grinned, finishing his dinner and reaching for her bowl. "Netting will keep the 'poisonous critters' out." He rose and took the bowls out, presumably to have them cleaned.

When he came back, she was retying her shoes.

"Going somewhere?"

"Just want to make sure I'm ready to run away in the night if a snake gets in."

"You think you can sleep with the threat of a snake hanging over your head?"

"I think I could sleep through a tornado right now." She crawled into the bed and pulled her blankets up to her chin, no matter how warm she already was. Her exhaustion was increasing the closer she got to sleep. "Tomorrow. We'll start observation tomorrow. For real. And talk more. I think you should try to think about the differences in your sleeping situations. See what might be causing you stress back home."

He made some sound of affirmation, but she didn't open her eyes to try to see what his expression could tell her. Or what he was doing as he moved around the tent. Preparing for bed? Making them safe from poisonous creatures that might bite or sting them?

This would be just like sharing a room with Jamison or her roommates in college. So he was handsome. So even thinking now about his kiss made her lips tingle and gave the sensation of movement…of hurtling forward without any semblance of control.

She wanted sleep. Her body craved it, her mind felt dulled by exhaustion and wrung out from riding that crest of fear for days straight. No doubt the reason she could only think right now about the physical sensation of his mouth on hers. That was easier than more intellectual pursuits.

The sound of his blankets came so close by… If she opened her eyes, he'd be just there, within arm's reach. In the stillness, if she listened closely, she could hear him breathe.

That shouldn't comfort her.

She rolled over, putting her back to him in the hope of calming her mind enough to drift off. She needed sleep. Lots of sleep. She could probably sleep for the rest of the week and not feel recovered…

# CHAPTER SIX

*KHALIL KNEW THIS blasted landscape. He knew every movement, every sound. He knew what he said. He knew what he did...*

*And this time he had to stop it.*

*To his left, he could see the stooped form of his brother, running in the night.*

*Already there? Already running?*

*Khalil pushed himself in the direction Arash had run, weakness crawling through him, dragging his effort down into sluggish half steps. It was the poison he knew he carried. It made him into something he didn't want to be.*

*The farther he ran, the faster he moved, even beyond reality.*

*Before Arash took that final step Khalil reached him, grabbed his arm and spun him around. As he opened his mouth to speak something lashed forward from behind him, a segmented limb tipped with a barb that dripped poison.*

*One quick movement, right through the heart, and Arash crumpled to the ground at his feet.*

*He didn't need to turn around to identify its source.*

*He was the poison. He was the betrayer.*

*He was the scorpion who'd killed his brother.*

Khalil knew he was in a dream before he pulled himself out of it. It was different this time, but the message remained. All his fault. All his fault.

His thundering heartbeat in his ears, sweat drenching his clothing more than it had even during the day's construction, he sat up and climbed immediately out of the bed, as if it were something that hurt him. As if he'd find it full of scorpions.

When he'd moved the few steps away from it that he could while remaining inside the tent, he remembered that Adalyn was there. With the darkness inside the tent he was lucky he hadn't stepped on her. Had she awakened? Had he said anything to make her wake up? When he found the light, would he find her looking at him? Find those lovely green eyes full of compassion, or something worse?

One thing was certain, he couldn't face that until he got control of his body, slowed his heart and breathing, but it was harder to banish the nightmare images when all he could see was the darkness. The blackness made a perfect projection screen to revisit his crimes.

To hell with her reaction to his nightmares. He had to get a light, get real images to fill his vision again.

He stretched his arms high over his head to feel the top of the tent, and from there and the slight breeze at his back that placed the door, he followed the tent to the side, where he'd find his lantern.

The battery-powered lantern clinked softly as he picked it up and fumbled about, searching for the switch.

Soon the tent interior was cast in low blue LED light.

He looked toward Adalyn's bedroll.

Not sitting up. Not looking at him.

He stepped closer, moving around to her

side of the tent so he could see if she was actually awake. It also put her between him and his abandoned bedroll—the thing that held approximately the comfort for him as a briar patch in a sandstorm.

Her features were relaxed in sleep, soft breaths, the slow rise and fall of her chest as she lay there, now sprawled on her back. The blankets she'd covered herself up with had been strewn to the side, revealing her in the khaki pants and top she'd worn into the desert that day, her boots still on.

Since it had been later in the day when they'd gotten the tent erected, the sand where they'd set up still carried heat from days baking in the sun. The tent walls held in this heat—gentle to the air but warm beneath, like a morning bed after a night with your lover.

She hadn't heard him. She hadn't witnessed anything. He pulled his shirt over his head and went back to his bag, intent on at least changing into something dry. Get rid of the reminders of the dream.

Now that his heart had slowed and ceased

bruising his chest from the inside, he could think about it. This one had been different. Where had that scorpion nonsense come from?

It hadn't happened that way, of course. That wasn't how he'd—

Adalyn. She was afraid of poisonous desert things getting into the tent in the night. But she'd gone to sleep with the most poisonous thing in the desert lying an arm's length away from her.

Ignorance was bliss for a reason. It certainly made it easier to sleep.

Think about something else.

What would she be doing if she were at home right now? The time difference meant…she'd probably be asleep. Sleep specialists tended to do most of their sleeping in the afternoon so that they could observe patients at night.

Did she live in a house or an apartment? Did she walk to work every day?

Did she spend her time with someone special?

Khalil had never doubted Jay's devotion to his little sister, though the way he spoke of her had led Khalil to think of Adalyn as the most boring woman in the world. He didn't even know what state she lived in.

Admittedly, this opinion of her as boring had probably been formed when they'd been teenagers and she had probably still been in pigtails.

Boring didn't fit her at all now.

The next time anyone tried to send him to a medical professional of any sort he was going to have to ask for a picture and maybe a phone interview before he committed to it.

And definitely not take anyone else into the desert with him to disturb his sleep.

Something had made the nightmare come to his safe zone. It couldn't be that he'd been thinking about it to summon it, because he thought about that night all the time.

Guilt maybe? For failing to come up with a story that would keep her safe before he got her to the desert? For not outright forbidding her from coming with him?

For kissing his best friend's little sister?

For the way her bed with its cast-off blankets looked like heaven, and his wet mess looked like some special kind of spiky hell?

Would the nightmares come back if he crawled into that soft, cotton paradise beside her and slept?

She'd wanted his kiss…

She might even welcome him into her bed… but the best she could give him would be a bit of oblivion. She could offer him no absolution.

He plowed his hand through his hair and pushed his blankets to the side of the tent so he could sit there.

No more sleep tonight, and he couldn't bring himself to check the time. It was still dark, so what did it matter how long the rest of the night was? Hours stretched before him any way he looked at it.

If he could just get through tomorrow, when night came again he could drug himself. The pills were in the truck because he hadn't expected to need them. If he went banging the doors around now to get them, he'd wake everyone in the camp.

With the battery-powered lantern in hand, he fished a book out of his bag and settled in to read. Staring at her peaceful sleep wouldn't do him any favors. Too little sleep had left his will-power shot, and if he watched her much longer he'd crawl right in beside her. The idea of sleeping with his nose buried in her hair and her soft body against him…. God help him.

He found where he'd left off and began to read. At least this way he could get into someone else's head for a while.

When they got back to the palace he had to send her home. And tell Jamison this was all something he had to work out on his own. It was foolish to think anyone could fix this for him. Even if the nightmares were gone tomorrow, it wouldn't change the past.

And, besides, maybe they were a gift. Something to keep him doing what he was supposed to be doing. To be the leader that Arash would have been.

A good man wouldn't need reminders, but maybe he did. At least these nightly remembrances kept in the front of his mind the kind of man he was, and the kind of man he needed to become.

Forgetting would only make his crime worse.

*  *  *

Sounds of life outside began to seep into the tent. In the desert people were early risers—outdoor work was best done before the sun reached its hottest and that suited Khalil's sleepless schedule. Fewer hours alone with his thoughts. The sounds actually began before the first rays of the sun hit the tent, before even the diffused pre-dawn light made it inside.

He should wake Adalyn.

Her bed and the peaceful expression on her face had tempted him every minute of the long night.

Still not daring to return to his bedroll, he finally dropped the book he'd read and reread all night, his reading comprehension not the greatest when his mind had been focused nearly entirely on the desire to sleep, or the desire to sleep with her.

The heat from the sand no longer really warmed the rug beneath him. But if he lay there long enough he'd fall asleep. At least for a few minutes. And when the dreams came again, since they'd finally found him in his safe haven, this time someone would notice. She'd wake, find him sweaty and panting, or worse—maybe he'd say something in his sleep.

Getting up and getting moving was the only way to get through this day.

Pulling himself up from the rug required nearly more strength than he had in him, but once he was up he dressed and fished a caffeine bean from his bag to pop into his mouth. He needed to get water to wash, tell the men to set up for vaccinations, check on Nadim again...and then he'd wake Adalyn.

Twenty minutes later Khalil set down a jug of water beside a basin where a towel and washcloth had already been placed, then went to crouch beside her.

She hadn't moved an inch in hours. Did she always sleep that deeply, or was this just the effects of jet lag? Maybe she had some magic pill to make sleep better. Something other than the ones he'd been using to self-medicate and hold on.

"Adalyn." He said her name before touching her hand, then said it a few more times, each repetition increasing his frustration, until he finally gave up the gentle approach and shook her arm until she opened her bleary eyes. "It's time to get up."

Sleep jealousy, what next?

"What time is it?"

"Early. Just after six." He gestured to the basin and stood. "Wash up and meet me in the other tent. We'll have breakfast together before we see patients. And we need to run two line-ups today—one for examinations and one for vaccinations. I will run examinations, you can do the vaccinations. We need to make sure everyone's healthy before they have the injection."

She nodded and sat up, her hair still smoothly braided from the day before… She really hadn't moved much last night.

"Did you sleep last night?"

Khalil nodded, even as his conscience made him aware that he was only answering the literal truth, not the truth she was looking for. He had slept—you didn't have nightmares without sleeping—he just hadn't slept much. "I slept." Not a lie. Technical truth was all he had going for him.

Tonight he'd get the medicine from the truck before everyone bedded down, and he'd have a whole dreamless night to catch up on sleep.

"How is Nadim?" she asked, apparently satisfied enough with his answer to move on.

"Much better. He even ate a little last night and everything stayed down."

A sleepy smile was his reward, and he turned to leave, intending to give her privacy to wash, but his foot caught on something and he felt himself falling but couldn't work out what to grab to steady himself. He crashed into the trunk, the corner smacking him in the solar plexus before he bounced off.

"Kha— Zain! Are you okay?"

He rolled onto his back, sucking in a painful breath and staring hard at the top of the tent, which spun in dizzying fashion.

Well, that had woken her up. Adalyn scrambled to his side and reached to touch his forehead. "Can you breathe?" His hair was mussed, and though it was already warm outside it wasn't hot, but he was sweating more, compared to the way he had been yesterday when he'd come in from tent construction. "Are you sick? Did you drink some bad water!?"

The shrill note in her voice startled her and she took a breath and held her tongue as she watched him work his way back into a normal breathing pattern.

If he got sick, she would just have to make Suhail and Hakem call for a helicopter to take him away to the hospital. And she'd have to ride back with one of them. For possibly the first time in her life Adalyn regretted never having learned to drive.

"I'm not sick," he mustered after a long, tense minute. "I just got…wobbly. Got up too fast."

"You weren't sitting. You were standing the whole time."

"I crouched beside you to shake you awake." The words came out gruffly as he rolled to his side first and slowly sat up. "I am probably a little dehydrated."

"Then you should drink something." She looked over at the jug he'd directed her to. "Is that water clean for drinking?"

"Yes, but I'll get some. You wash and meet me there."

He didn't look good or even moderately steady, but Adalyn didn't argue as he shuffled toward the tent entrance and through it.

*Shuffled* was the right word. His feet barely left the ground as he walked, which was probably why he'd fallen. Nothing to do with standing up too fast and getting dizzy. He walked like a zombie, the mindless locomotion of someone truly exhausted.

He'd lied to her. If he'd slept at all last night it had only been for a few minutes—maybe an hour at most—but she doubted it.

Great. She should have tried to stay awake long enough to observe him. She'd just been so tired, which made her all the more sympathetic to his current state—as if she didn't already have years of experience with the aftereffects of sleepless nights.

Adalyn washed and dressed with record speed, and headed for the other tent to eat and observe Zain-Khalil.

As sleep-deprived as he seemed to be, he really shouldn't be seeing patients.

With the small population of the village Adalyn reckoned they could've gotten the vaccinations done in a day by just running one line, but this was Khalil's show, his decision.

His sleep-impaired decision.

Giving shots didn't take much brainpower, and her mind wandered along with her gaze over the tent. Not many men had turned up, mostly mothers and their children. One set in particular concerned her. The little one lay against her mother's shoulder limply, asleep. She couldn't have been more than five—if she was that—and she was definitely ill.

So when Adalyn turned back from the station where she'd prepared the next vaccination and found that same mother and the now awake child waiting, she began to realize just how impaired he was from sleeplessness. Putting down the vaccine, she went to Khalil's station a few feet away, picked up his thermometer and stethoscope and headed back to the mother and child.

Khalil gave her a look but she ignored him. After a few short motions to explain to the mother what she was doing, she put the thermometer to the child's head and had her suspicions confirmed. Fever, low grade for now, but signs of infection. With her borrowed stethoscope she listened to the child's belly and sighed. Had he even listened? From everything Adalyn had heard from Jamison, Khalil was observant and conscientious, not the type to be lax in his duties to patients.

Motioning for the woman to wait, she took the instruments back to Khalil and leaned in to whisper to him, "That girl is sick. She can't have the vaccine. Did you listen to her belly?"

"She's hungry."

"And the fever?"

"It's hot outside."

"No," Adalyn said, tilting her head toward them again. "Ask them to come back over. I don't want to look like I'm questioning your authority, but that girl can't have the vaccine." She paused for a heartbeat, but before she could really think about whether it was right to do so in front of

others she went on—they probably couldn't understand her anyway. She whispered, "I think
you should have a nap in the tent while I'm here.
Let me handle the examinations and inocula-
tions. Hakem can help me with translation."

Khalil frowned, but rather than arguing with
her about the girl he took his instruments and
had a listen to the child's belly again. After confirming her quick diagnosis, Khalil spoke with
the woman and sent her out of the tent with an
electrolyte-enriched drink for the girl and medicine for nausea. While not as ill as Nadim had
been, she'd still need to be watched.

That frown stayed with him as they finished
up the last of the vaccinations, which took con-
siderably longer than the first half—which told
her he was slowing down and trying to pay more
attention.

The problem was that trying to pay better attention didn't amount to much when you were
severely sleep-deprived.

As they were packing up the instruments Adalyn
heard some commotion outside and before she

could ask Khalil what they were saying a man with a head wound came rushing in with a little girl in his arms.

Hakem moved before she could even ask what was going on and had a table out for the man to lay the child on.

Adalyn met Khalil at the table, grabbing instruments as she went in the hope of helping.

The girl's skin had a blue cast to it. Adalyn's throat seemed to close up. This was an emergency, far more so than the one they'd had with Nadim.

Words flew back and forth as questions were asked and answered.

The girl's top came off and the bruise on the right side of her chest really brought the situation home for Adalyn. She didn't even need to palpate that bruise to know the ribs were fractured in two places—a section sucked in slightly with every labored intake.

Flail chest.

Khalil listened with the stethoscope, but the girl's breathing was so loud and wheezy Adalyn could hear it without the stethoscope.

She needed surgery. That was it. That was all that could help her...

So when Hakem handed Khalil a large-gauge hypodermic, it took her a couple of seconds to react. "What are you doing?"

"She's got a tension pneumothorax."

"No." Adalyn grabbed his hand to keep him from puncturing the girl's chest. "She's got flail chest. That needle isn't going to help her. She needs surgery, Dr. Zain. She needs surgery. Look." She gestured for him to look at the girl's side, where at least two ribs were cracked in two places, creating a floating section of chest wall and messing with her ability to inhale. "Do you have sedatives?"

"Yes." He looked confused for a moment, so Adalyn stepped between him and the table and said to Hakem, "We need to ventilate her. And one of you needs to call for the chopper. Now."

She left Khalil standing, looking even more out of it than he had, and went to his drug cabinet. Her hands skimmed over the glass bottles, causing them to clink and clatter as she found her way to the right drug. Grabbing a syringe and alcohol preps, she got to the table, found a vein and injected it. By the time she'd completed the shot and the girl started to drift off, Khalil had gathered his wits enough to retrieve the right sized intubation kit for her.

He didn't even try to do it himself, just prepared the instruments and handed them to her one at a time.

It had been years since Adalyn had intubated anyone, let alone a child. She began murmuring the steps to herself, making sure she remembered, and Khalil added a couple of tips as he tilted the girl's head back, doing everything he could to help her complete the intubation.

Less than a minute after she'd ordered Hakem to call the chopper she attached the bag and began forcing oxygen into the girl's lungs. Within seconds her color began to return to normal.

Hakem returned, taking over the bag. "You have to go with them in the helicopter, keep her breathing. She can't do it on her own. I'm going to set up an IV for her and send you another dose for when she starts to rouse."

Not her job. This was not her job. She wasn't

built for emergencies. Her knees wobbled, but her hands stayed steady enough to surprise even her.

"You've got things under control," Khalil murmured to her. "I'm going to go…to the tent."

Adalyn nodded, tying the tourniquet around the girl's arm and threading the catheter into the vein. "What happened to her?" she asked Hakem quietly.

"Car crash," he said, shaking his head, his voice lowered as he said, "It is harder to do out here… Unless you are reckless."

Cold shot down the back of her neck, as if this was the Arctic, not a Middle Eastern desert.

"I see." Her voice wobbled, just like her knees. She taped the IV port in place and then packed him a small kit with a couple of saline flushes, another two doses of the injection, because she didn't know how long it would take to get to the hospital, and she also didn't know how quickly they'd take the girl in even if it was an emergency. The best she could do was to overprepare, for safety. Grabbing a notepad from the back table, she made some quick calculations and wrote down the times Hakem could give the other doses needed to keep her under, then led him through it to make sure her instructions were clear.

"Is he her father?" She gestured to the man still at the foot of the table.

Hakem nodded.

"Tell him what is happening. Can he go, too?"

Hakem nodded again, and before he could start talking she said, "Broken ribs, and maybe a bruise on her lung."

Since she was there, she got together the supplies to bandage the man's head—butterfly closures would have to do, since he refused stitches. And Adalyn was kind of glad. She really hadn't stitched anyone in ages. Today had been a day for revisiting too many old, rusty skills.

And she still had Khalil to deal with.

## CHAPTER SEVEN

HOW HAD ADALYN become the village surgeon?

Sweat—having nothing to do with the heat—still plastered her shirt to her back.

Hakem had called for the helicopter to pick up Adila and her father, which did relieve her a bit. At least now she knew Hakem would have someone to mind the bag if he needed to give another dose of the sedatives she'd sent with him. But having the tent free of patients meant she was now obligated to find Khalil and choke him to death.

She barged through the flap in the tent and found him sitting with his back against a trunk, the only solid thing in the tent, staring into space.

"Zain." She snapped her fingers and he lifted exhausted eyes to her, but the shell-shocked expression in them sucked the anger right out of her. "Did you sleep at all last night?"

She grabbed the bag he carried on his visits to Nadim and went to kneel in front of him.

He sighed and nodded. "I did. I just don't know how long."

With the sun still high, the white interior of the tent was bright enough for her to examine him.

"Are you having memory lapses?"

He watched her as she dug the stethoscope from his bag and put it around her neck. In his satchel, she spotted the plastic bag full of coffee beans but didn't comment on it. Yet. She knew all the tricks to staying awake.

"How would I remember that?"

"Don't be cute, Khalil." She whispered his name to keep it from traveling. Khalil was her patient, not this Zain alter ego. She needed him to really hear her and would use whatever weapon she had at her disposal. "How much did you sleep?"

"Not much."

"What woke you?" She pressed the listening end of the stethoscope to his chest to listen. Elevated heartbeat. "You're chewing the coffee beans, right?"

He sighed, waited for her to listen to his heart and then nodded.

"Your heart is going like a horse at full gallop. You can't have any more of those."

"They're helping me stay awake."

"Yes, and that isn't helping you." She dropped the instrument beside her and repeated the question he'd not deigned to answer. "What woke you?"

"Adalyn..."

"No, Adalyn didn't wake you. Adalyn slept through the whole night and probably didn't move once or make even a single sound." She was speaking about herself in the third person, which was kind of even annoying her. "Something woke you. Bad dream? You need to tell me the truth now." She snatched the bag of coffee beans from his satchel and shook it at him. "People who have insomnia don't need help staying awake."

"Bad dream." The two words came out softly, but perhaps not by choice. His words rasped, as if they had been forced out, and he had only barely managed to get his voice working at all.

She stuffed the coffee beans into her pocket and laid a hand on his cheek so he'd look at her. "About the war?"

"About the war."

All he'd done was repeat her words, but the haunted look in his eyes told her everything she needed to know. She wouldn't ask him for specifics about the dream. They weren't important at this point anyway. What was important was getting rid of all his crutches. "What else are you using to keep from them?"

Whether he took comfort from her hand on his cheek or just didn't have the energy to push her away, Adalyn couldn't say, but it became too much for her—the dark stubble on her palm sent electricity scratching up her arm. She slid her hands to one of his and took it instead, keeping the connection but trying to lose some of the intimacy that made it hard to think.

"You mean to stay awake?"

The fact that he needed to ask for clarification on what he was using to keep the nightmares at bay told her he was doing more than just trying to stay awake.

"To stay awake, sure, but anything else?"

"Just normal things."

"Pills?"

"Not really. I've randomly taken a steroid or two in the past couple of months, but nothing… nothing regular or, you know, prone to cause addiction. I didn't need to. I was leaving for the desert every few days. Exercise, extreme doses of caffeine, keeping busy…they all helped until I could get back out to the desert again. Frequent short trips."

He was talking and she needed to keep him talking, so she prompted him whenever he even hesitated slightly. "But last night was different?"

"I guess. I really don't want to talk about it, Adalyn. I just want to try to sleep again. Maybe you could sleep in the other tent. Or maybe I should sleep in the other tent—your being in the tent with me is the only difference I can think of."

"No. You're staying with me." She'd had at least enough sleep to carry her through one night, so she'd be the one awake tonight, making sure he didn't stay up or sneak more coffee beans.

She stuffed the stethoscope back into the bag. There had to be some way to help him through this out here. They couldn't leave tonight. They should leave tomorrow, early if they could, but she wasn't letting him drive anywhere, and she didn't know how to drive, so she couldn't do it. He had to sleep tonight. She'd seen the aftermath of badly driven vehicles just half an hour ago…

"You need at least four hours tonight, and we're going to swap out some of your crutches for others."

The flap opened and Suhail came in with the night's dinner—a repeat of last night's, but made freshly, thank goodness. Before leaving, he wordlessly handed a bottle of pills to Khalil and left.

Khalil opened the bottle and shook one out, then reached for his water.

"What are those?" Another crutch? She set her bowl down and grabbed the bottle of pills, and then the hand he'd shaken one into so he couldn't take the darned thing while she was investigating. Flipping the bottle around, the logo on the cap made her stomach bottom out. "Have you taken these before?"

"Not often. Once per visit at home, that's it."

"So the last time you had one?"

"Three or four days ago."

She set the pill on the other side of her and shook her head. "You're not taking them."

"I need to sleep, Adalyn."

"Yes, you do, and you also need to wake up again. These never passed FDA approval, which I know means nothing to you here outside American review panels and such, but the reason they didn't pass is present, no matter where we are. You know the trials? You know how many people died? If you're suppressing dreaming, I can understand that, but you can't do it with these pills. There are others. There are some that are almost through trials and much safer."

He pulled his hand free to take it anyway, and Adalyn did the only thing she could think of... and tackled him to the ground. "You're not taking these!"

The shock of her leaping on him and knocking him on his back worked in her favor. Khalil dropped the pill…and spilled his water. With reflexes enabled by rest, she scrambled off him, snatching the pill from the bedding before he could recover.

Without pause, she darted out of the tent with the pills in her hand. The heat sucked the life out of her, like always, but she found Hakem and thrust the pills into his hands.

"Zain—" she said the fake name, getting his attention "—cannot take these. Even if he asks you for them, don't give them to him. In fact, please get rid of them somehow."

Hakem looked at the bottle, a frown pulling down his heavy brows. "He needs them for his insomnia."

"He needs them like he needs a hole in his head." She shook her head, took a breath and rubbed a hand over her face. "They're not safe. They can cause uncontrollable bleeding. So, even if he asks you, don't give them to him. You're here to protect him? Save him from these. Get rid of them."

Hakem answered with a slow nod, enough that

she took it as a win for now, and turned to head back into her tent.

She found Khalil sitting on her bed—since she'd doused his in water—scowling.

"Eat. Then I'm going to examine you again. And then you're going to sleep." Let him scowl. He could look however he wanted as long as he listened to her.

"What did you do with them?" he asked, ignoring her orders.

"I buried them in the sand somewhere you'll never find them—even if you dig a thousand and one Arabian holes in the desert."

She kicked off her shoes, grabbed fresh water to hand to him and then sat beside him to eat.

"You think something has changed in the past five minutes since you examined me before?"

"I wasn't looking for signs of bleeding before. Bruising. Or what I'm really afraid of…" She looked at the top of his head and then looked him in the eye again.

"I'm not having a hemorrhagic stroke. There would be symptoms."

"We'll see. Those things have a ridiculous

half-life. If you had them three or four days ago they're still in your system enough to mess you up. Not enough to help with the dreaming, obviously, but that kind of bleeding isn't something that can even be controlled. Why did you pick that particular drug? There are safer ones that are almost through the trials."

"They wouldn't ship them here."

"Why?"

"They thought we were trying to steal the formula or something. Make generic ones. Who knows? I couldn't get an answer, and I didn't raise enough of a fuss to get one, because I didn't want the attention. All they had to do was leak something to the press and——"

"And you wouldn't be able to hide this." Adalyn understood hiding nightmares, and when she'd done it she hadn't had the weight of an entire country riding on her shoulders. Somehow, sharing fears brought a kind of vulnerability unlike anything she'd experienced in her life. That was a big part of why she wasn't digging further into his nightmares. Well, that and it wasn't her job.

Generally, she was the first step in getting someone to a good therapist to deal with whatever trauma was causing their nightmares. And although she knew Khalil wasn't going to go to a therapist, she didn't feel equipped to help him on that front. All she could do tonight was treat the symptoms and try to get him some sleep before he suffered some kind of psychotic breakdown.

Whatever he was thinking, he gave up speech and focused on eating. At least she didn't have to tackle him again to make him eat.

They ate in silence, and once the dishes had been removed she fetched a jug of water, a couple of washcloths and a basin, and came back inside.

The sun sat low on the horizon, and the white tent no longer glowed with light. She set her washing supplies to the side, grabbed his kit again and fished out the penlight.

Khalil had moved the trunk to her bedroll so he could lean against it again, and she knelt in front of him to shine the light in his eyes.

"This is unnecessary."

"Says you, and your judgment is terrible today." She made him look at her and checked pupil reactivity. "Good. Okay. Take off your shirt and your pants."

He lifted one brow.

"I'm going to look for signs of bleeding. Bruising. I'm going to feel your belly. And you're going to tell me about your bedtime rituals. What do you do when you're trying to fall asleep? Do you think about it? The nightmare?" She avoided referring to the cause of the recurrent nightmare for now. And in order to keep herself from staring at him as he stripped, she went about moving his wet bedroll and opening hers up so that it lay flat and they could both lie on top of it.

"I try not to think about it." Despite the looks he'd been giving her, he followed her orders. The shirt came off. Then the T-shirt beneath it. And finally he stood and unbuckled his pants and let them fall away. "What are you doing?"

She shook the sheet out and laid it to one side. "When you're trying not to think of it, you're actually thinking about it. Your brain doesn't remember the 'no' part of the thoughts. It just focuses on the nightmare. You're priming yourself to have it by trying not to have it. You need distraction, and we need to change your sleep environment for that."

When she'd futzed with the bed until she could futz no longer, she grabbed her perfume and sprayed once over the blankets.

"What are you doing?"

"You said you liked the way I smell, so I'm... I thought it would be nice. We're going for comfort and things that please here," she said quickly, then tossed the bottle onto her bag and focused on him again. "I'm going to look for bruises. You can wash your face and whatever. Get rid of some of the grit. It'll feel nice. And that's the whole point, to feel nice and comforted and different. Oh, yeah, I didn't mention it before... You're going to be sleeping in my bed with me."

The other brow joined the first, halfway up his forehead. "You think that's a good idea?"

"I'm not offering sex. And your bed is wet, besides. Do you... When you..." She cleared her throat, grabbed the light and went to shine it on his arms first, tracking over the skin to look for darkening. Clinical. This was an examination, not a sexy striptease or whatever. *Think of Khalil as a patient. No. Think of him like Jamison.* That should be sufficient to keep her from having inappropriate thoughts during the examination of his admittedly really, really nice body.

Not something she should be noticing. *Focus. Get the stupid question out and then get on with whatever didn't require enough concentration to talk.* "Have you been…with anyone, you know, since they started?"

"You mean have I slept with a woman since I've had nightmares?"

"Yes." Of course it was easy for him to put the sentence together, and he was the one who was sleep-deprived. She moved on to his chest but looked much more quickly so she could move around to look at his back. "Have you, and…has it helped or…you know…anything?"

She sounded worse than her idiotic twelve-year-old self when she'd gotten around a boy she'd liked. Adults talked about sex without getting flustered and stammering.

"I haven't been with anyone since then, no."

"Okay. Well, I guess it will be an experiment. I'm going to be a stand-in…bed friend. But not in a sexy way." She sighed and dropped to look at his feet, then his calves. Calves got banged up all the time. The dusting of dark hair on tan skin made her job harder, never mind the dips and bulges of muscles casting shadows. Bruises stood out better on her, being so pale. That was why this was taking so long. Not her distraction. She was just being thorough.

"So, anyway, just…we'll do that and see how that goes."

She looked at his thighs even faster than she'd looked at his chest…because she wanted to slow down and look longer. When she was satisfied he wasn't bruising randomly, she made him lie down and did a quick examination of his abdomen for any hardness or signs of bleeding. Nothing. Nothing but a knot in her throat and a headache from the way she couldn't force her eyebrows to relax.

Pulling away, she poured water into the basin, washed her face and then handed him the dry cloth and towel. "I'll sit with my back to you if you want to wash a bit…and then I'll wash a bit…" Good grief, this desert trip was such a mistake. Hotel. She was supposed to get a hotel room with a bathtub and air-conditioning! And she was supposed to see Khalil only in a clinical setting with machines…and cameras…and colleagues!

And now that she knew what he was up against, she couldn't even enjoy wishing she hadn't come. Those if-only gateway thoughts to more pleasant mental vistas even made her feel guilty.

If she hadn't come, would little Adila have survived today? Would Khalil really have been able to sleep last night if she hadn't been there, and been more clearheaded today? If she'd caused his lack of sleep, then that mistake was only because of her being there.

Maybe she had made things worse.

Or maybe he'd keep taking those pills and would suddenly bleed to death while bending over to pick up something from the floor because the slight pressure change made a blood vessel in his brain burst. That drug was a nasty thing. Foolish. Desperate…

Khalil watched Adalyn sit with her back to him, as she'd announced she would, and went to the basin. The sooner he got this over with, the better. Thanks to his performance today, the idea of her figuring it all out no longer seemed like the worst thing in the world.

Maybe she would figure out what he'd done, or maybe having her soft skin against him would bring the kind of comfort that had tempted him all last night... Tonight, at least, his guilt had nothing to do with her and everything to do with his own choices. Being in the desert might be his biggest crutch, but he never would have relied on it if he'd even suspected he wasn't providing good care to these people. Now he had to ask himself how many other faulty diagnoses he had made while this mess had been going on. How many bad decisions was he making regarding the kingdom?

That meant more than his pride.

Besides, what could it really matter what she thought about him? It's not as if he'd ever see her again after she left here.

The thought made his shoulders tense, and he had to roll them a couple of times as he washed, the tension itching deep in his bones.

"Do I have doctor-patient confidentiality with you, Adalyn?"

She didn't turn around, though her head tilted slightly, an indication that she was not only paying attention but examining everything he said.

"Of course you do."

"I don't just mean with the press and strangers, I mean with everyone. Jamison. Or even my men here with us."

"You don't have to worry about it," she said, and then fell silent in a way that said she was chewing on something else. He let her chew on it, got dressed in fresh clothing and went to sit beside her on the bed.

When he sat, she looked at him. "I asked if you're dreaming about the coup. The war zone you went to. You don't have to tell me what the dreams are about...but are they about something that happened there? I'm not going to ask for any other details, even though I do think you should find someone to talk to about the dreams and their cause. And that's all I'll say on the matter tonight." She twirled her finger around and pointed at the tent wall in the same direction she'd been facing.

She was going to wash.

And that'd undoubtedly involve taking her clothes off...

"Yes." He said the word quietly, swiveling as instructed to face the tent wall. It was just as well. Knowing his luck, he'd fall asleep in the middle of making love to her, and she didn't need him giving her more issues.

"Do you remember when I told you that I had nightmares after the crash?"

She was going to talk to him...while he was supposed to be watching the wall. Made it harder to stop himself from turning.

"I remember. How long did you have them?"

"About two years. At first, I didn't want anyone to know. Because I knew they were wrong. The things I dreamed weren't what happened at all. And at the time people said I became hysterical all the time. I really hate that word, by the way. They need to come up with another one that doesn't imply big emotions being related to ovaries, or negative traits associated with having ovaries."

He grinned at the little tirade, but something she'd said earlier stuck with him. "What do you mean, you dreamed what didn't happen?"

"A couple of weeks before their wreck there was a very close call and I was in the backseat of that one. But in my dreams the two events somehow got mashed together. My imagination played a big part, because I remember being in their accident. I wasn't in it, but the memory I have is so emotional, it feels real…"

He felt her sit behind him and turned to look at her. She'd stripped down nearly as far as he'd done, tiny white cotton shorts and a matching top with straps. There it was again, the look of an oasis, cool and refreshing.

"Does it bother you to talk about it now?" he asked, trying to focus on what she was telling him rather than the way he wanted to mash himself against her and lose himself in her scent.

"Not really. I talk to patients about it, but I don't…I've never really told Jamison. He was away at school, and he seemed to need that sep-

aration. I felt like if I told him he'd come home
to be with me and it all felt very selfish. Now I
don't tell him because I know he'd feel guilty for
not having come." She lay down and patted the
bedroll beside her in invitation. "I don't know
how you usually…you know, lie with a woman.
And you probably shouldn't lie that way anyway.
We're making things different but still comfortable and comforting. So I feel like I should be
touching you somehow."

Khalil looked at her a moment longer, then
stretched out the opposite way and rested his
head on her belly. "Touching." But any wayward
erections in his sleep wouldn't traumatize her.

And it wasn't enough. He pushed the hem of
her vest top up enough to expose her midriff and
laid his cheek on her belly again, and this time
the cool, soft skin against his face was enough
to pull that tension from his shoulders.

Her breathing came a little shallower, and
Khalil was glad he'd turned so his gaze was
down toward her feet and not up at her breasts
and face. "I'm not sure this is going to work if
you can't be comfortable."

"I can," she argued, and then he felt it, a tentative touch at first, but she began to comb her fingers through his hair and he nearly fell asleep right then. "Feels kind of like a scene out of *The Arabian Nights*."

"Why's that, Scheherazade? Going to tell me a story?"

"I was thinking about it," she said, and then firmed up her answer, the combing continuing. "Actually…yes. You need something new to think about when falling asleep, and I know a good story for that."

It was true, he did need to think about something else. He didn't tell her that he'd been thinking new, consuming things since she'd lain down beside him. Hearing her talk could only help— he was tired to the point that it wouldn't keep him awake, but her voice had a soothing quality. She probably did this with other patients, maybe not exactly this, but changing their sleep schedule, maybe even the gentle, distracting conversation while they fell asleep. And there was something altogether sweet about her telling him a bedtime story when any other woman who'd made it to his bed would be angling to dazzle him with sex.

"So, I'm going to tell you a story about the dream warriors and the dragons..." she said, the gentle tone of her voice fading as he immediately began to drift off, one thought sticking with him: whatever dragons lurked and waited for him, she was ready to charge into that battle in his stead.

# CHAPTER EIGHT

ADALYN BECAME AWARE that the big warm body that had been close to her all night was gone. And there was a sound of movement in the small tent.

She opened her eyes to pitch blackness and fumbled around at her side for the lantern, flipping it on.

Khalil was on his hands and knees, his shoulder stretching out the side of the tent, he'd moved so far away from her.

His eyes were open…and his T-shirt stuck to him, drenched in sweat, but he didn't look awake. People could do all sorts of things in their sleep, but over the years Adalyn had cultivated the ability to spot the differences. Acting strangely aside, there was something missing in the eyes when consciousness was an illusion.

Would he respond to his fake name if she said it? Probably not.

Normally she wouldn't wake someone in a nightmare, she'd just let them go through it and monitor what happened with her equipment. But she'd promised to stand guard tonight. She had to risk saying his name and hope he didn't come out of it swinging.

"Khalil?" She said it low, crawling toward him in what she hoped was a nonthreatening manner. The way his muscles strained and the wideness of his eyes said that whatever he was going through was bad enough.

She said his name again, and then just started talking, picking up the thread of the story she'd been telling him, the one that she'd listened to herself repeat a thousand times when wrestling with her own night dragons. Every instinct in her said to touch him, ground him to reality and the moment with her, but that instinct was wrong. Dangerous, until that hyperalert expression faded to the inevitable confusion that would follow when he actually did waken.

"Khalil?" She said his name softly again.

Nothing. If anything, he looked more strained than he had. Even in the low light and with his soaked T-shirt rumpled on his skin, she could see the muscles down his spine and over his ribs bunched and tight.

She couldn't risk saying his name louder, so she tried something else. "Adalyn." She said her name, once…twice…and this time she did touch him. First just stroking her fingers over the back of his hand, then up his arm, then to his cheek… By the time she'd combed her fingers through the damp black hair, he'd fully woken up.

The confusion she'd expected wasn't there, but he did go from looking dazed to grim before she could think of anything to say.

Pulling away, he stood and walked to the opening of the tent, unfastened it and stepped directly out into the cold night air and the open sand in his wet shirt and shorts.

Adalyn gave him a moment. He was awake now, and not in any danger out there.

The danger was in his mind, and she'd promised to protect him from it. Despite her assertions that she'd had sufficient sleep to stay awake the whole night, she'd failed. If she'd stayed awake, maybe she could have gotten him out of it before he'd become soaking wet and panting.

Her plan to change Khalil's sleep experience by changing his surroundings and rituals had seemed to work, at least partially. Probably until she'd fallen asleep and had stopped talking to him. Which was why she should never have told him the story she'd conditioned herself to go to sleep to—her brain took it as a sign that it was time to sleep.

Right.

Cold air blew through the opening…enough to cool her down. He must be freezing. And maybe embarrassed. She couldn't just leave him standing out there indefinitely.

She stood and followed. He'd not moved from the opening, just stood outside the tent. "Hey, come back inside." She touched his arm again, and he turned to look at her.

The moon, bright and full, illuminated the landscape, and her eyes adjusted quickly enough, having been in complete darkness before. "I'm sorry, this was my fault. I fell asleep on you. It's probably not much comfort, but I'm fully awake now. You can try again…or we can just get you out of the wet shirt and you can come inside, relax an—"

A low tone came from nowhere, stopping the words in her throat, almost like a bell that just kept ringing. "What is that?" she whispered, stepping slightly closer to him.

When he didn't immediately answer she stepped fully out of the tent and up beside him, slipping her hand into his.

"It's a dune," he said finally, and even if it didn't make sense to her, him talking about anything was a good sign and she wanted to keep him grounded there with her. Help him let go of all the bad feeling that tended to cling after a particularly bad dream.

"I didn't know they did that. They don't do it in the daytime?"

"They do." He flexed his fingers so that hers settled better between them. Piece by piece, word by word, that's how she could help him right now. And besides that, her curiosity was roused.

"But they weren't ringing yesterday."

"They only do it when there's a slide. Like an avalanche but smaller and of sand. Happens when the wind blows the top ridge off a steep dune and the sand spills down one side."

The bright moon made it possible to see him, but she couldn't see his expression as well as she had with the blue lantern. And she really needed to look into his eyes right now, figure out whether he was upset about the dream or angry at her for failing him. He moved his arm, pulling out of her hand, and looked out over the desert and the outskirts of the village where they'd set up.

The tone finally started to fade, and she was starting to get cold. "Please, come back inside." His name was on the tip of her tongue, but she managed to keep it there while outside the tent, even in the middle of the night. "You're going to freeze in that wet shirt."

Khalil turned to head back inside, pulling off the shirt she'd objected to once he stepped into the tent again. Two nights running he'd have to down another bottle of water before morning at this rate.

Adalyn closed the tent behind him and went to feel the bedroll. "It's pretty much dry. You must have gotten up before you really got drenched." She rolled onto her bottom and sat, cross-legged. "Do you want to talk? Do you want me to shut up? I promise to stay awake this time. I'm really sorry…"

"Don't be sorry," he finally murmured, and went to sit beside her, not bothering with another shirt this time. He had only one clean shirt left and if he put it on and went back into the dream, he wouldn't have an undershirt for tomorrow. "It's not your fault. You can't control my subconscious."

"But I don't think you were having a bad dream when I was talking. Only after I fell asleep." She turned her arm toward the light to read the dial of her watch. "You did very well for the first two hours. The last time I looked at my watch was about an hour ago. So it was after I fell asleep that the dream returned."

"Circumstantial evidence," he said, then leaned

to the side to grab a bottle of water. "I'll try again. Maybe we can change things. I'd rather lie up beside you, but I've no intention of pawing you."

The word *intention* made that statement the truth. He had a strong *desire* to paw her, and kiss her, and blot out all the ugly thoughts still lurking at the black edges of the tent, but resisting that had to be his number-one priority.

He tilted the bottle to his lips and drained it in one go. Definitely dehydrated, his throat felt like the singing sand.

"But if I lie down, I might fall asleep again."

"We'll risk it." He screwed the cap on again and then gestured to her. "Lie on your side, whichever side you prefer."

She lay on her right side, and then looked at him…brows up and perhaps a tiny bit of nervousness showing in her eyes. Khalil crawled over her to lie down behind her and tucked her smaller body against him. If she was as innocent as all the blushing and stammering suggested, she probably didn't have much experience of spooning with a lover. For some reason that thought pleased him even as he doubted it could possibly be true. That stupid inner caveman of his.

"Just relax, go back to sleep. We both need it. It takes a few days to get over jet lag. If you managed to stay awake for a couple of hours, you did more than your part." He slipped one arm under her head so that her head rested on his biceps and the other around her waist, but what he really wanted was more of her scent.

He hadn't been talking about her perfume when he'd complimented her scent before, even if that's how she'd chosen to take it. The perfume was nice, it had been distracting at first—which had been the point—but it was that special Adalyn smell he wanted. She had some earthy sweetness he'd never be able to define beyond pale, generic words. She smelled good. Fresh. Maybe a little salty even. He burrowed his nose in her hair and closed his eyes.

She smelled like a cool breeze blowing off the sea.

Good God, she smelled good.

"Isn't my head going to crush your arm?" She

whispered the words, as if they were going to get caught and get into trouble. As if he hadn't already told people she was his mistress.

"If your head gets heavy, I'll move my arm." Her back was stiff against him. "Is this uncomfortable for you?"

"No. I'm just…not used to being touched a whole lot."

Of course she wasn't. He let his hand fold over her hip and pressed her back against him, squeezing in a way he meant to be comforting, and maybe a little flirty. "Want me to tell you a bedtime story so you can sleep?" With her pressed against him, it was hard to remember she wasn't what he'd told everyone.

The tease made her chuckle. "No. I'm going to sleep on my own like a big girl."

"Got it, no story." He could sleep like this. Maybe she'd relax better after he'd gone to sleep. "Don't move away from me when I fall asleep."

"I won't," she whispered, and with slow, deliberate effort began to relax. He could track her thoughts as she did, almost hear the muscle groups echoing in her brain as she focused on them one at a time, starting with the neck and letting his arm support the full weight of her head. Then down her shoulders and back. When she'd willed her body into submission, she laid her arm over the one at her waist and squeezed his hand, "Sweet dreams, Khalil."

It sounded like a blessing when she said it.

He stretched his fingers back until she took the hint and slipped hers between them.

With their fingers linked, he fell back to sleep.

Adalyn treated sleep like a cross between a business and a holy experience. People who'd had sleep issues in the past—the kind that left a mark—tended to do that.

Don't stay in bed when you've woken up or it teaches you to lie in bed awake.

Don't do anything in bed but sleep. Well, maybe one other thing, but she hadn't branched out into that other bedroom activity.

Though now, waking with Khalil behind her, his arms around her and his slow gentle breath fanning her neck, she had to wonder why.

The second thing she noticed? He was still asleep.

There was nothing she could do to keep the smile off her face. It may be unconventional medicine—and even that was minimizing how wrong it generally was—and while she'd truly never want to do this with another patient, it felt nice with Khalil. It felt natural.

A quick look around informed her that the sun was rising, even if it hadn't yet fully risen—the tent had taken on the soft gray cast of indirect light filtered through white canvas.

She should let him sleep a little longer.

Slowly, she shifted forward, intending to slip out of his grasp, but his arm tightened, pulling her back against him.

"No."

He said one word, then pressed his nose back into her hair and the deep breathing resumed.

How to deal with this?

Adalyn checked her watch. Not quite six in the morning. People started the day early here—she could already hear movement in the village—but it felt mean to make him get up so early.

"Are we driving home today?" she asked softly, since he'd had the rule about getting on the road at six. And if they had to take the tents down, they'd never make it before ten if they didn't get up immediately.

His legs stretched out behind her, but he kept his arm anchored around her waist. "Yes."

As he nuzzled closer, she felt the brush of lips and stubble against her neck.

Had he kissed her neck?

She stilled, her breath stopping as warm, feathery kisses moved up the side of her neck and chills crashed over her.

Did he remember it was her sleeping with him?

Was he really awake or did he think he was in bed with one of his past lovers?

Heaven only knew what was going on in his mind. If she'd had him hooked to her equipment, she'd at least be able to tell if he was dreaming or if this was a conscious action.

But this was a no-equipment zone, and with him behind her she couldn't even look him in the eye to tell.

She shifted beneath the weight of his arm until she was on her back and could see him.

His eyes were open, and a little amused.

"Are you awake?"

"As far as I know," he murmured, and then slid his hand up from her waist to cup her jaw, tilting her head just so… Leaning in, he continued those featherlight kisses over her jaw to capture her mouth, light and teasing until her breathing sped up and her lips parted, then the gentle kisses became something altogether more insistent. More luxuriant. More sinful.

His bare chest right there, hot against her side, his long bare legs tangling with hers.

One second she was thinking about getting up and getting to work, and the next her arms had crept up and around his neck, holding him to her so he wouldn't stop kissing her.

Again she had that sensation of movement, but unlike every ride in a vehicle of any description that she'd ever taken since she was twelve this movement only brought a rush of excitement.

His hand slid up her ribs and cupped her breast through the thin jersey knit of her tank top, the gentle kneading building another kind of tension in her belly. An ache that started as a squirm, then got needier.

His two-day beard growth scraped her cheeks and chin, hot and rough against the smooth softness of his lips.

They could be a little late…

It took every ounce of willpower Khalil had to keep from stripping off those tight shorts, ripping off the top that separated him from her breasts and the hard little nubs begging for his mouth.

Last night his exhaustion had overridden everything else—it had felt like heaven to have her against him, but now that his exhaustion had been battled back somewhat, his mind and body craved more of her sweet sanctuary, whatever form it might take.

Her hands plowed into his hair, holding his head to hers, while one of her legs tracked up the outside of his—an unspoken invitation. He could have her. She wouldn't want him to stop… He just had to get the material out of the way.

His hands shook as he slipped them under her,

squeezing her soft cheeks as he lifted and hooked his fingers in the waistband of her shorts. One little tug and they slid past the curve.

Where was the sheet?

They'd been warm enough in the tent, tangled together to forgo the sheet, but he felt blindly behind him now and dragged it over them so at least, if anyone came barging in, she'd be covered.

"Khalil..." From her lips his name sounded like a plea, and his heart thundered harder, faster.

She hadn't called him Zain and he didn't correct her.

Zain wasn't the one invited into her embrace.

He dragged her shorts the rest of the way down soft supple legs, dropped them and immediately went for her top, as if it was a race. As if every second that a barrier existed between their flesh might actually kill him.

He needed her. He needed this.

He pulled the top off, exposing to his gaze small, perfect breasts with desperately pink, erect little peaks. The need driving him kept him from looking longer. Leaning in, he took a nipple into his mouth and sucked hard. She arched into him and he let his hands roam, learn her curves, pull her closer.

"Dr. Zain," a man spoke. They weren't alone…

Something else was said, and he didn't catch it, his attention immediately focusing on covering Adalyn. He grabbed the sheet and dragged it up, and only then did he look for the person who'd spoken.

There was no one in the tent.

But that had been Suhail's voice. Outside the tent flap but very close.

*Hell.*

In a louder voice Suhail spoke again, and the tenor told Khalil he was repeating himself. Time to take down the tent. Everything else had been done. Time to go…

"What's he saying?" Adalyn's soft question pulled his attention back to her and the dazed look in her lovely green eyes. Right, she didn't speak Arabic.

"We need to get up." A short summary was all he could manage, still leaning over her, their flesh pressed together from torso to toes. Still hard and heavy against her hip.

Her dazed expression was the sexiest thing he'd ever seen.

Wide eyes, pink cheeks and an impossibly throaty whisper. "We were going to have sex, weren't we?"

Okay, it was the first time he'd ever been asked that...

Khalil nodded, not sure how to take the question.

Adalyn swallowed, licked her lips and focused on his mouth with demanding intensity. "I still want to."

Thank God.

"Me, too." The words came even as he dragged himself away from her. "But it's bad timing. I'm sorry, but Suhail may have saved us..."

*Get up. Get dressed.* The longer he lay there with her, the less likely he'd get out of that bed for a few more hours.

"But you said you wanted to." She sat up as he stood, clutching the sheet to her chest as she did.

"I do. But I don't have any condoms with me. We weren't just about to have sex, we were about to have unprotected sex."

* * *

Adalyn's gaze fell to his erection and whatever arguments she'd been about to make died in her throat.

There she sat, clutching the sheet to her chest, and he strode around without a shred of shame.

Lord, it was sexy.

Was this what he felt when he looked at her?

She dropped the sheet, letting it pool at her waist. Not quite so far as strolling around the tent completely naked, but a step.

His eyes slid down with the sheet, and she watched the muscles in his abdomen squeeze, the proud member bobbing in response.

She'd done that to him and it made her want to do more. To stand up. To test his resolve to get back on the road today. All bad impulses, but all she really wanted to do.

At least at this moment he wanted her as she wanted him. He may have been with a whole caravan of women in his past—she really had no idea and had no desire to ask—but right now he wanted her.

Her.

Plain little Adalyn Quinn, easy to overlook and even easier to forget.

The realization came in a heady rush that made it even harder to ignore the brand-new ache low in her belly.

The whole situation overrode all logic and rules about safety—things she prided herself on and used as her first and most important guides in life—but if he came back to the blankets with her she'd take the risk. She'd revel in the risk, if it was even only just as good as being kissed by him.

If he hadn't turned away and begun getting dressed, she might have even begged… How was that for risky and vulnerable?

Her weakness really should worry her more than it did.

"Don't go out there yet," she whispered as he approached the tent flap, shoes in hand, and she scrambled out of the sheets to come up behind him.

"Adalyn, I can't. We can't. I can't be in here with you." He turned, and though he glanced down at her body, it was quick and he locked onto her gaze again.

"Do you regret this?"

*"No."* His denial came with enough force to banish those niggling voices. "But I have to go." A soft sigh came and he looked back at her. "You look…"

What? Sad? Turned on? Terrified?

"Since the moment I found you dressing you've looked like an oasis to me." He shook his head, taking his time and looking at her now, and as his eyes skimmed over her body he reached out and let the back of one finger track down over the small swell of her belly, a brief touch that caused a fresh wash of goose bumps. But when he once more looked into her eyes the heat there banished any lingering fear or chill. "This isn't over."

Three little words kept hope alive…

Before she could find any words to say he slipped out of the tent.

It took another several breaths before she calmed down enough to wash up. If he could get on with the task of packing up, she could, too.

She just couldn't do it with the scent of him clinging to her and keeping that flame burning bright in her chest.

# CHAPTER NINE

ADALYN SPENT THE ENTIRE drive back to the palace alternating between two conflicting emotions: fear and arousal.

With Khalil there beside her, the air-conditioning may have cooled the actual air but the current running between them still sizzled and popped.

Though she might not want to admit it, picturing him standing proudly naked before her, flushed and panting and looking at her as if he could do things to her that she couldn't even imagine, was entirely too good a substitution for the usual bloody, awful death scenes that filled her mind when she travelled.

And right now that meant she'd fixated on his shoulders and the strong, lean arms that stretched to the steering wheel. He had nice shoulders. Wide and sturdy, without being overly bulky. Was it weird to obsess over shoulders?

"Stop it," Khalil said, his eyes on the road.

"Stop what?"

"You keep looking like that, and I'm going to pull over and finish what we started this morning."

Because she was staring…

"I can't help it," she whispered, smiling despite her breathless confession. To play down the want running her ragged she laughed a little. "You're better to picture than broken, twisted bodies in burning metal carnage."

"Well, that's a relief."

She grinned wider. "Not by much, but…" This feeling. This was why people flirted and played with one another. And to think, all this time she'd kind of thought she was just…not interested in any of this.

Khalil heard her breath hitch. It'd be easy to think that it was just because she was replaying their morning and not that she was afraid of the drive still, but he really couldn't tell which way her attention was going. She had a thing about using the right crutch at the right time to deal with painful situations. Sitting there, staring at him, could be a crutch.

And he was going to mess it up.

"Not that I want to make you suffer by reliving bad memories, but something about what you said about your nightmares has been bothering me."

She looked back out the side window, the playful tone going out of her voice as she said, "I can talk about it. It's okay. It doesn't really hurt me now. Other than, you know, the worry that someone will think I'm a little unhinged if I tell them the truth about the situation. But I think you understand…"

But she'd stopped smiling.

He understood being ripped apart by nightmares, if that's what she meant. But rather than dig into that, he asked the question burning in his mind. "What did you mean when you said that you remembered their wreck?"

"Well, memories are thoughts, right?" she said, and when he nodded continued, "If you picture something repeatedly, your brain learns it just like it learns a memory. It can't tell the difference. That's the whole basis behind brain-washing—manipulating the natural manner of learning and memories."

"Yes." Something still didn't gel. "So your nightmares were you reliving these false memories you'd given yourself?"

"Yes, but I didn't know they were false. I still..." She paused long enough for him to look at her. Whatever it was she wanted to say wasn't coming easily. Maybe he shouldn't make her do this.

"It's hard to explain." She gripped the seat belt and tightened it as she spoke. "I know I wasn't there. I know it. I know exactly where I was when it happened. I even remember being there. But...I also remember being in the crash, even though I wasn't there. All I have is emotion, and the emotion of that memory is so strong that it overrides reason and what I know to be true. It even seems clearer to me before I start looking for details."

Khalil knew there was something in what she said that he was supposed to get, but he didn't. "You don't have details in your fake memory?"

"I have some details, but… In the real memory I can tell you exactly where I was, who I was talking to and even what we were talking about when the police came to tell me about the crash. But it feels distant. I know now that's because of shock, but the fake memory feels more real because it came later, when the shock had worn off. It has the fear and emotion but it doesn't have the details."

"What details?"

"We always listened to music in the car, but I couldn't tell you what was playing. I couldn't tell you what my mom was wearing before the crash, or where it happened. I couldn't tell you the color of the other cars involved. And when I realized that, that's when what really happened started to seep back in, contrary to what I'd pictured over and over. It was there, but even today it feels less real to me."

He nodded. "Why did you picture it over and over?"

"I don't know. Because I was twelve? Because of the smaller wreck a couple of weeks before? I'd been in that one, but we were on the periphery of it. Other cars got the worst of it, and our car only got knocked on the front left wheel well, and the driver's window shattered beside my father's head…but we didn't get hurt. Not really. Sore for a few days, but not hurt. The other cars, the ones that actually caused the wreck? There were several people inside those vehicles, and only a couple survived." She looked back out the window, and Khalil could tell that the fear was starting to replace whatever mellow mindset she'd made by looking at him.

"Look at me," he said, reaching across the cab of the truck to take her hand.

"No… No, you need both hands on the wheel!" She pushed his hand back to the wheel, the pitch of her voice rising.

"Okay, but look at me," he said, taking hold of the wheel with both hands now, in the ten and two positions, as he'd been taught. "You don't have to tell me anything else. I think I get it. You saw what happened to those cars, and then, when they wrecked, you knew enough about how it would play out to picture it."

"And I couldn't stop obsessing over it. I couldn't

stop wondering how long they'd lived after the crash. Had they been waiting for help to come? Had they been praying and trying to comfort one another? Wondering who would take care of me and Jamison? Had only one of them been awake, or alive? Had one seen the other slipping away before they succumbed, and known they couldn't do anything to help?"

She'd said it couldn't hurt her, but her voice got weaker the more she led him through those questions, breathless. Sounds of pain...

"I had so many questions, and they were all terrible. My aunt and uncle—that's who took us in after it happened, my mother's sister and her husband—well, mostly they took me in, because Jamison was away at school except for the summers. Anyway, they thought that by not answering those questions, not talking about it, they could save me from it. But they couldn't."

"Did you let them help any other way?"

"Yes. I asked them to send me to therapy. There had been a couple of visits with a grief counsellor for two weeks after, but it was only enough to make even my twelve-year-old self know I needed someone better," she answered, and then shrugged. "Because I knew it was wrong. I knew I was messing up somehow, but I didn't know how else to handle it. By the time I'd gotten in to see the therapist, I'd already picked the vision of the crash that best appealed to me and reinforced it to the point of madness. In my memory now they died at the moment of impact. But I can see their bloodied bodies, I can see…glass shards piercing their faces, the engine pushed up between them, crushing them. I see it like a picture, a snapshot. Like it's real. No suffering. Just gone. At the same time. Whenever I started to worry or wonder…that's what I pictured. It was a terrible thing that happened, but…"

She stopped in mid-sentence, then fumbled for her water to take a long drink. *Wash it away, the emotion, the images…* It definitely still ate at her. That kind of emotion was impossible to fake. She really did feel she'd been there, even though she knew she hadn't been.

He didn't know what to say.

"So I messed myself up by trying to picture the only scenario that made it the tiniest bit better. The way the mind works is amazing, and sometimes terrible."

"Did you ever find out how it actually went?" He shouldn't keep making her talk about this, but he knew she hadn't told Jamison any of it. Her brother, the person she was closest to, didn't know. If she didn't tell him, had she told anyone but that therapist? Did she talk about it at all anymore? Maybe she needed to.

A soft sniff demanded he look at her again, but she'd closed her eyes and was busily swiping her cheeks with her hands.

"I... No. I didn't. I don't know what would happen if I found out and it was worse. Sometimes you just have to let go of things that you can't change. I can't make it a kinder story, and I accept that, but I'm afraid that if I find out it was worse...the dreams would come back. That I'd obsess, that I'd trigger some kind of psychological avalanche. So I walk softly around it. I saw a therapist until we got through the constant nightmares. She was the only one who knew, so you can believe I know all the unhealthy tricks to hiding nightmares."

"How long did it take?" he asked, brushing past that little warning she'd given about hiding his own.

"I don't consider myself cured, Khalil." The words came softer than the others, the same voice he'd use to break bad news to a patient or their family. "I'm...I'm in remission. Sometimes I relapse, and I have a CD I play when I'm sleeping for when that happens. Posthypnotic suggestion has been the best maintenance plan for me. And it took me two years to get through the worst time."

"What's your CD like?"

She smiled again, shaking her head. "It's me telling myself a bedtime story."

"Dragons and dream warriors?"

"Yes. That's part of the CD. The first part. The last part is me repeating what actually happened that day for me, not them... One's kind of soothing, and the other is me trying to bolster the signal strength of what actually happened. Beef up my own real memory with the repeated words... It goes on for about twenty minutes. When I first got the idea for that I was already practicing. Every morning when I went to bed after a shift in the sleep clinic I wired my head up with electrodes and ran them to a monitor. Then the next evening I reviewed it all, came up with an average time that it took me to fall asleep and built the recording times around those averages. And now I only use it until a nightmare phase passes and things return to normal."

"Why doesn't that trigger more nightmares?"

"I don't know. I think because it happens when I'm asleep. If I'm having trouble falling asleep and that part of the CD begins to play, I stop it and get up for a little while, then go back to bed and start it from the beginning. I don't listen to the suggestion part when I'm awake. Not since I recorded it."

"I don't understand what any of this monitoring is going to tell you. We've already established that I have nightmares that interrupt my sleep."

Khalil sat on a high stool as Adalyn painstakingly placed electrodes on his chest. The closer the actual time to sleep approached, the more he hated this idea. The only acceptable part of the whole situation was Adalyn standing so close and constantly touching him as she applied one monitoring device after another. Every innocent brush of her fingertips distracted him enough to keep him sitting there…at the tipping point between falling asleep where he sat and dragging her to bed to make damned sure he had a good night.

"I want to know at what point in your sleep cycle your nightmares are occurring," she said, pulling his attention back to the fact that she was cocooning him in wires. "You can't tell me that, since you never seem to know how long you've been asleep before they start."

Her sweet breath fanned his skin as she leaned in close for different steps in her task.

Touching her would make him feel better, but he was now awake enough to recognize that wasn't a great idea. It was both a fantastic idea and a terrible one. They'd both agreed to cool things down when they reached the palace, so his sleep could be as normal as possible. Adalyn wasn't the type to have a fling, and hurting his best friend's little sister—especially when she'd come all this way to help him—didn't sit right. His libido was less than convinced it was the right thing to do, but he was ignoring it.

"You need to monitor my heart for that? I can confirm for you that it does race when I'm in the nightmare."

She looked up at him, making eye contact only long enough to confirm that her thoughts were also somewhere else. The closeness affected her, too. That shouldn't please him.

"I know it does. That's why I need to monitor it. Increased heart rate is an indication of fear, as is the amount of sweat on your skin—and I have monitors for that, too. As well as respiration. Your heart will speed up before you start to sweat, but it's all valuable data. Indications of when your nightmares are starting. What point in your sleep cycle."

He didn't need to ask about the EEG, the cap with all the wires she'd hung on the camera until it was time to strap him into it. "Do you do this to people with insomnia?"

"Yes."

"They're already having a hard time getting to

sleep. All this discomfort…" His complaining started to scratch along his own nerves. When complaints turned to whining, it wasn't a good look for anyone. Just take the wires and electrodes and get on with it.

"I know. You aren't going to have that problem, though. I bet I could put a dancing monkey in the corner and you'd still be able to sleep within minutes of hitting the pillow, you're so sleep-deprived."

"I slept a few hours last night," he reminded her.

"And you have a sleep deficit. You can't make up for all that missed sleep and the stress it puts on your body in a couple of hours. Now hush. This is to help you. You want them to go away, don't you?"

"Yes," he muttered, and closed his eyes as she shook out the cap with the leads and tugged it onto his head. What he must look like. Ridiculous.

She buckled the strap under his chin, tested the tension and then dropped one finger to the waistband of his pajama bottoms, tugged it out a few times as if testing the stretch of the waist.

"What are you doing?"

"Just checking to see if you've got your cranky pants on."

Khalil wanted to glare at her, but he captured her hand instead, his thumb pressed to the pulse point on her wrist. "Do you want me to take them off? I'm happy to take my pants off for you, Adalyn." He could play games, too. Only, his were more fun.

Her cheeks immediately went pink and she gave a little tug to free her wrist from his grip. "Not unless you like to sleep pantsless. This is all about your comfort. That's why I'm making with the cap instead of loose electrodes that I have to hold on with tape and a wad of conductive goop. It's much more uncomfortable." She turned and picked up a large, blunt-tipped syringe. "Almost done, and this is less goopier than the other EEG getup. Just one more thing after I'm done with the cap."

"That is?"

"Straps around your belly and chest to measure respiration, and an electrode on your legs to measure movement. Oh, and the sensors that track eye movement."

"That's three more things."

She tilted his head this way and that, the needle going into the cap at regular intervals… hitting all the different electrode ports on the cap with a conductivity compound. Not only was he wired up, he was gooey. And gooey was anything but sexy.

He should get some kind of reward for putting up with this.

When that was done, she performed the last three quick steps and then carried all his leads to the bed so he didn't trip on them. A camera on a tripod sat at the end of the bed, along with some panel that received the other end of all his wires. She ushered him into the bed before plugging him up.

"If you need anything, just say my name and I'll come running."

"You're going to wake me when they start?"

Adalyn paused as she looked at him, trussed up like a Thanksgiving turkey. If she said no, would he still go to sleep? Probably not. She could tell him yes, but it would be a lie. She needed as much data as she could get, and that meant she needed him to stay in the nightmare as long as he could. He might be having small warning nightmares that led up to the big one, kind of like aftershocks to an earthquake, but before. If she woke him from the small ones…

· "I'll wake you if you look like you're in great distress. That's really the only way that I'll know that you're in a full-blown nightmare. Otherwise you might be having some other exciting dream. Because there are different phases of dreaming, and the phase you're in when you have them is important to treatment."

"Why?" Despite the scowl he wore while lying there, his eyelids had already started to droop, and the word was no sooner out of his mouth than it stretched into a wide yawn. Poor baby really was so tired…

"Because different cycles of dreaming have different jobs. It's all your brain trying to process memories and new experiences and make sense of what information you've been feeding it, and when those dreams occur matters. It helps

identify what your subconscious is trying to figure out. If we can provide those answers when
you're awake, then we have a much better chance
of controlling those dreams."

It was true, but not the whole answer. And he
still didn't look pleased about it. But, then, when
did he ever look pleased about anything when he
was being forced to go to sleep? Only children
and adults with nightmares fought sleep, the rest
of the adult world fantasized about lying in bed
for long lazy hours, a reward for the exhausting
trials of modern life.

"Let's just get on with it." He closed his eyes
and rested his hands on his belly. When she went
to pull a sheet over him, he waved it off. "I don't
want it."

Rather than making him even an iota crankier,
she turned on the camera at the end of the bed,
turned off the lights, turned on her flashlight so
she didn't trip and headed to her suite…where
all her monitoring equipment was set up.

Adalyn wasn't a liar. She didn't sugar-coat things.
She was honest, and damn the consequences.

Usually.

She also wasn't the sort of person who spent vast quantities of time with other people who were actually awake. There were a few people at work, those who spent enough time with her to know her quirks and like her anyway, but other than that she leaned much harder toward straight talk than gentle reassurances.

And, still, given all that, she'd lied to Khalil.

Nothing was ever conclusive where dreams were involved, but his nightmares while in the palace were so predictable, there was an extremely good chance that she could tell when he began having those dreams again. People dreamed almost the whole time they slept, but the worst offenders happened during REM sleep. That, coupled with his physical reactions, should be enough to let her know when they started.

Had she told him the truth, he'd be up chewing coffee beans and refusing to cooperate. It all left a bad taste in her mouth. As did her entanglement with him. There was nothing professional about the way she looked at him. The way she felt. But for all she knew, maybe this was just how it was for most people when they were attracted to one another. There could be nothing special about her feelings, except that as a romantically underdeveloped adult she just didn't have enough data to categorize it all.

Quietly, she sat through the ninety-some minutes it took him to get there. As soon as the brain waves changed she picked up her flashlight, moved everything out of the way and waited. She didn't want to go in until he was waist deep in it…

The other part he would have objected to: she wanted to wake him only when he was so immersed that his defenses were down. It was the only way she'd get answers.

The sensor began picking up sweat on his chest, and she prematurely silenced the alarms there, clicked on her flashlight and tiptoed into the suite so she could stand in front of the camera and actually see him go through it.

Not that she actually wanted to witness it. His frequent anger and grumbling was a bit more understandable to her than it probably was to anyone else.

The sympathy she felt for him probably made him more attractive, too. And she really did want to wake him now, but who knew if he'd give her another chance to observe him?

People with sleep issues tended toward heavier activity during sleep. The usual sleep paralysis didn't always fire right with them. His legs were moving, as were his arms…and his breath sounded so loud in the cavernous dark.

Her eyes began to burn.

So loud, so fast…she couldn't wait anymore. Stepping around the camera, she came right up to his side of the bed. She switched the flashlight to her other hand and did what she shouldn't do— she touched him. Just one hand, gently lighting on his shoulder. "Khalil?"

He came instantly out of the bed, wild-eyed and shouting words she didn't understand. The next instant he'd sprung from the bed and knocked her to the floor. Her breath whooshed out of her as he landed on top of her and sent the flashlight flying from her hand.

As she struggled to suck in a painful breath beneath him, the light—wherever it had landed—flickered and went out.

He flattened himself over her, pinning her to the floor, and said something else.

Her lungs burned now, too. "Khalil? It's me. It's Adalyn. You're okay."

He shushed her and whispered, finally in English, "Stay down."

The weight of him wasn't inconsiderable, and he'd captured her hands to hold them down, too.

She'd seen people come out of nightmares swinging, but she'd never seen them come out of nightmares…like this.

He was protecting her…

"Khalil, it's a dream. You have to wake up." She tried to pull her hands free from where he'd pinned her, but his hands gripped her wrists tighter. In the utter darkness she couldn't even see him. She couldn't tell if he was waking up or not. She tried something else. "I'm safe. I'm down. You've got me."

The grip on her wrists loosened and she slid her arms around his shoulders as a deep, terrible trembling racked him. "It's okay." She whispered now, too, petting the back of his neck, uncaring about the wires she'd trussed him up in. For a moment he pressed his face against the side of her neck and let her comfort him.

She was supposed to be asking him questions, but she'd already learned so much.

He was definitely dreaming about the war.

He was trying to save someone...

And then she knew... In his dreams, every night, Khalil tried to save his brother.

# CHAPTER TEN

FOR SOMEONE SO unused to physical affection it was remarkably easy for Adalyn to pet and console Khalil.

He needed her and, having seen his face in the throes of his nightmare, she needed it, too.

The shoulders that so enamored her shook with the tension lingering in him, but her hands glided over smooth skin, stroking and kneading as she whispered assurances.

It was a dream.

Everything would be okay soon.

They were safe in his bedroom, where things were soft and sweet, not the war she didn't mention, even if her always overactive imagination supplied her with images of explosions, searing heat and flying metal. Of Hell.

But it was more than that. Touching him, holding on to him, felt more necessary than anything she could ever remember. It was important. And not just that, but it roused equal parts of protective instincts and need. And the small taste she'd had of him wasn't enough. Might never be enough.

Even this wasn't enough, but she'd stay there beneath him as long as he wanted.

Something brushed the side of her neck and awareness shot through her. It was an accident. Someone just out of the throes of a nightmare wouldn't be kissing…

His head moved, his mouth glided up her neck with featherlight brushes to that hollow beneath her ear. Then something hot and wet… His tongue.

Adalyn's heart surged into a dizzying pace and her lungs, only just recovered, sped up in concert. She opened her mouth to say something, but all that came out was a breathy stutter, all sounds and no pattern. Thoughtless sounds.

Khalil took the sound as a request, and soon his mouth was on hers, hot and vibrant, firm and needing. Strong, despite that terrible wound he carried.

He wanted her, and it felt right. It felt fierce and free and absolutely necessary if she wanted to maintain her sanity. She'd heard that hormones could make people stupid. And she didn't care. She was going to do something stupid, and it felt brilliant.

Moving her hands from his glorious back to his head, she pulled him back long enough to fumble off the chin strap and pull off that ridiculous wired cap.

Khalil took this as an invitation and she felt him lean off her, the darkness of his bedroom so complete that she couldn't even see his outline in the dark.

But she heard wires pop free from his electrodes.

She heard the plastic click of the strap on his chest and then his belly.

He was stripping.

She rose to her knees and felt his face, pulling off the taped-on sensors.

No sooner had they freed him from the monitors than strong arms came around her hips, clamping her to his chest as he rose. Even in the dark, even after his lips once more found hers, he managed to get them onto the bed. She felt the softness give beneath her as his firm heat pressed her down.

One of his hands, strong and just slightly roughened by his labors in the desert, slid under her shirt and up over her ribs. It started as a tickle that made her smile into his kisses, but ended in a full-mouthed moan as he dipped beneath her bra and stroked over her puckering nipple.

"I can't see you." He whispered the words against her lips. "If you want me to stop, you're going to have to say something out loud."

Adalyn shook her head and then managed to get some words out. "Don't stop." That was all she could manage. He leaned away and before she knew what was even happening in the dark he'd dragged her slacks and panties off. She ripped off her top and the bra beneath, and by the time he'd leaned back into her on the bed she could feel the length of him down her body, and everywhere they touched her body bloomed with sensation.

It seemed he touched her everywhere, his hands, his mouth, and she felt the nip of his teeth over her hip.

204 FALLING FOR HER RELUCTANT SHEIKH

As his lips and tongue passed over her thigh he murmured something in his own tongue. She didn't understand, the only thing she picked up on was the sensuality weighting the word.

"Come back…" she whispered, blindly groping for his shoulders to urge him back up over her. Adalyn had read the medical texts, she was familiar with the mechanics. She expected pain, and she didn't care about that, either.

He settled between her legs and she slid her hands to his hips to pull him against her, certain that if he didn't take her soon, the ache that had steadily grown since the very first touch of his lips days ago might consume her.

Khalil wished he'd turned the light on. After a nightmare the dark had always been a canvas to continue his mind playing out the nightly torment. It didn't have a chance with her touching him, beneath him, but he still wanted that connection… To see the look in her eyes when their bodies finally joined.

Next time. He couldn't stop long enough to find the light.

Gripping himself, he brushed the head of his erection along the heated folds of her sex. Finding her ready and his patience at its end, he found her entrance and sheathed himself inside her.

She made the smallest sound and froze, her sex clamping down on him like a toe-curling vise.

He wanted to move but couldn't when the realization came that she was in pain. For all her blushing and shyness he'd never really thought that the innocence about her was actual innocence. "Adalyn…" He whispered her name, then started to pull away from her. Light. God, he needed the light.

"No…" she said, grabbing his arms and pulling him back to her. "Don't go. I'm sorry. I should've…"

He leaned back into her and settled. It took every ounce of will to give her the time she must need to become used to him.

"I'm okay," she whispered, pulling his head back down to hers, her sweet mouth moving against his.

"Tell me when the pain is past…" It felt wrong to say the words out loud when the room blanketed them in darkness and he was so attuned to her that her every sound broke the air like a shout.

She flexed her hips against him. "I think it's gone already." She tested her control of those sleek internal muscles, each squeeze driving him closer to the edge of madness.

He began to move. Too fast, no doubt, and too hard… His control was shot. His conscience, overused of late, reminded him that this was wrong. Wrong for her, wrong for him…and he ignored it. He'd take whatever wrongness she deigned to give him, and thank her for every second of it. For every touch. For every whimper. For every sweet touch that gave him relief. That made him feel alive.

Whatever remained of his willpower gone, he could've cried for the joy of feeling her climax begin to ripple through her. Before the last spasms faded, his own erupted and he emptied himself into her. His pain. His grief. His seed… The last realization came with another ping of his conscience. Something he couldn't think of now, it would have to be tomorrow's burden.

She still lay trembling beneath him, and he wanted her to stay with him in the bed. Hooking one arm around her waist, he dragged her up to the head of the bed, letting himself slip from her so he could stretch out beside her.

"Khalil..."

"Stay." He said the word that mattered to him right now. He needed her to stay. Not to hook him back up, not to wait for more nightmares to come. He just needed her.

Somehow the nightmares didn't enter into it. They seemed so far away at that moment, no doubt some of her light spilling over him...even in the darkness. And he'd take that, too.

She turned to face him and snuggled in at his side. The abandoned electrode on his chest bothered her cheek and she flicked at the corner, ripped it off and then nestled her cheek on the smarting patch of skin.

"Sweet dreams." From her lips, would those words always sound like a benediction?

"Khalil..." Adalyn said his name, focusing her mind on the subject she needed to talk to him about just as he turned the truck off the main road and into the unpaved desert. This drive was already better than the last one. Since he'd gotten men in to replace the glass she'd broken, the air-conditioning actually worked.

It had been nearly a week since that night she'd woken him. A stretch of nights in which he'd slept some every night. Although he had never slept the full night through, anything was better than the sleepless purgatory he'd been exiled to before her arrival. She knew he slept not because she monitored him but because she was always right there beside him. And when he woke up in the middle of the night he woke her, too.

"Zain," he corrected her, his voice remaining light as he reminded her that they were leaving the world of her patient for the world he used to escape his problems...

"Zain." She tried again—what to call him wasn't a fight she could afford right now, especially when she was still determined not to blow his cover. It wasn't exactly fair of her to make him have this conversation while he was driving—and the strictly rational part of her mind most strongly objected because making him talk would take his attention away from the road, where he should be focused. But talking would be the distraction that kept her from focusing on the fear in her belly. "I've been trying not to pry into the subject of your dreams, but I don't feel like that's something I can keep doing."

"Sure it is," he said, and slowly looked over at her in the seat beside him. "We have other things we could talk about. How delightfully hot and snug that…"

"Stop." She groaned over his words, "That's… distracting. I'm not going to talk dirty to you while you're driving in the desert." She wasn't good at dirty talk anyway, and that was part of his delight at her trying, amusing and arousing at the same time. And her ability to turn him on was like discovering some heady new superpower. She could get so distracted by him, so easily. She had to focus. This conversation needed to happen.

"You like to talk when we're in the car. It's a pattern with you. I'm just trying to help you think about something besides the truck."

"No, you're trying to make me think of something besides the subject of your dreams." She would stay on topic. She would stay on topic. "We're heading back to the camp…"

"Different camp." Another correction, though this time the levity in his voice had faded.

"Okay, we're heading to a different camp and you're not avoiding sleeping, but when we're together…"

"It's working. Us being together. I'm sleeping, I'm making better decisions than I was—I see that now. Having you with me…"

"But I feel like I'm your new crutch." She blurted the words out and let them hang there for a second as she watched his jaw flex and all traces of his playfulness disappear. "I'm not going to be here forever." Even as she said the words some emotions she didn't want to face twisted inside her.

Khalil was a very intelligent man, he knew that without her reminding him, but he'd been avoiding that subject. Which just proved her status as the new crutch.

She'd think about that later. She turned in the

seat, enough to look at him without abandoning her seat belt. "I know you were trying to protect me when you tackled me. You thought I was Arash, right? You're reliving the war when you couldn't save him?"

He drew a slow breath, before releasing it in a rather irritated way.

"Please, tell me. You need to talk about it, and I know you're not going to go to a therapist. You probably also aren't going to talk to your family about it. So that leaves me, Hakem, Suhail or Jamison. And I'm here now..."

"And you won't be soon," he said.

"Right," she confirmed, and then stopped. "But I'm not on a time schedule. I mean...I'm on indefinite leave, which is not to say that I can stay for months but we do have some time. And a couple hours' drive, right?"

Time when he didn't have any demands being made on him to run the country or save lives. Time he could use to save his own.

"I don't want to talk about it."

"Of course you don't, it's unpleasant, and sweeping it all under the rug is another crutch."

"A crutch? Like you distracting yourself from your fear of cars by talking? You want me to talk? I want you to drive." He took his foot off the gas and let the big truck slow on its own.

"I don't know how to drive."

"I don't know how to talk about this."

"Khalil…"

"Zain," he corrected again, turning to look at her as he applied the brakes and slowed the beast down. "You drive, I talk. That's the deal."

"It's a bad deal. I won't be able to pay attention to you because I don't know how to drive! I'll have to spend all my attention steering and—"

"There are no roads out here. You can't go off the road if you're already off the road."

"And we might not ever get there. What if I go over a big dune the wrong way and then the truck gets off balance and turns over and rolls down to the bottom and bursts into flames?"

"That won't happen. This isn't Hollywood. Cars don't burst into flames just because they roll over." He shifted into Neutral, then reached over and flipped open her seat belt.

"This is ridiculous."

"Well, this is the way it is."

The way it was… Him once again counting on her to not have the courage to do this. And if they had been back in New Orleans, or even in the city here, she probably wouldn't. If she'd not spent so much time traveling the past ten days, she probably wouldn't. She knew exposure therapy helped people, but she just had never been able to force herself to do it.

He stared at her, one hand on his seat belt, ready to fasten the thing again and get back to driving.

Normally, she'd never agree to this deal, but the longer they sat with the truck not moving, the warmer it became. The air-conditioning only worked so well out here. And he was counting on all these things to make her give in.

"Fine," Adalyn said, forcing a lightness to her tone that she didn't feel, and turning as she stood, removing herself from the seat so that he could slide into her space and she could step over into his.

The look on his face said he thought she was bluffing, and he slid over easily and fastened himself in.

She twirled and sat beside him, then scooted to the driver's seat.

Did he know how this pushed at her nightmare? Had she told him that being in the car wasn't enough for her imagination, that what came with that false memory was the kind of guilt that could only be called self-blame? As if maybe she could have changed the outcome if she'd done something before... Or false survivor's guilt... But guilt all the same.

The truck's engine still rumbled as she went through adjusting the seat with Khalil's help to slide it forward enough to reach the pedals. This, unfortunately, cramped his leg room, but that was just tough. If he was bound and determined that they both suffer as much as possible, then that's what would happen.

"Okay, how do I shift and make it drive?"

This led through a somewhat less eager period of instruction as Khalil began to realize she was really going to try to do this. That didn't mean that she'd be able to split her attention and talk or ask the right questions at the same time, but at least she was going to try to hold up her end of the deal. If this was the only way he would talk about his dreams…

Hakem and Suhail, who'd left a little later than she and Khalil, finally reached them and pulled up alongside.

Another conversation she couldn't take part in, and they pulled ahead, leaving them to Adalyn's driving to get them to the village.

"How far before they're outside the range of the radio?"

"Several miles."

Her stomach bottomed out. "Great…" No one would see if she crashed and they exploded. "Tell me how to get the gear to shift again."

It took another twenty minutes for her to get the truck up to enough speed to get it into the proper driving gear, and her nerves were well and truly frayed by the time she did it.

And she was supposed to talk to him now. Now that she couldn't remember what the heck she was supposed to be talking about. About his dreams. Confirming if her conclusions about what had actually happened were anywhere close to what had happened. And mostly…providing him a safe place to talk about it all.

Safe place. Hah. As if this was safe.

"You're going the wrong way."

"You said there wasn't a road so not to worry."

He tapped the GPS doodad on the dashboard. "We still have to end up at the proper coordinates to find the village."

She couldn't figure out how to manage one other thing, and navigating was it. "Screw it." She took her foot off the gas. "Downshift it for me and I'll get back over in my seat and you can drive the darned thing. You win. Let's hope you don't win the whole stupid war, because you'll definitely be the one to lose if you do."

Khalil did as requested, and once the terrifying vehicle stopped moving she unbuckled and climbed over him again, this time not bothering to stand and let him slide over—she just climbed over his lap after he slid a few inches toward her.

The maneuver had her straddling him at one point, hands on his shoulders for balance, but before she could lift the other leg to complete her walkover, he grabbed her hips and focused her attention back on him.

Suhail and Hakem wouldn't come looking for them anytime soon. No one else was going to roll up and catch them, but doing what they both wanted to do right now would just be rewarding his bad behavior.

Even someone as minimally experienced as she was could see desire flare to life in his eyes as he captured her in that vulnerable position.

"I swear to God, if you try to kiss me…" she muttered, but even as she said the words she had to wrestle with that little excited wiggle in her belly that wanted him to kiss her. And in order to make herself get on with moving, she pushed at his shoulders until he let her continue over him and he slid toward the driver's seat.

Once they were fastened in and he had the truck moving, and once again back on course, she said, "I drove for…lots of minutes. You owe me like…ten questions answered."

"No."

"Eight."

"No."

"You don't get how bartering works, do you?"

"You're in no position to barter, Adalyn."

"Seven, and I will state clearly here for you that you're definitely the bigger coward if you don't even try. If I'm the one more committed to your recovery than you are. Just so long as we're clear on that."

He looked at her, the corner of his jaw flexing. "One."

"Six."

Another of those long-suffering and irritated sighs escaped him. "Two."

"Five." She should probably be happy with two, but she was greedy for this information.

"Two."

"You're supposed to say three."

"You're supposed to just ask the questions."

"Fine." She twisted slightly in the seat again so she could look at him. "You tried to protect him, and when you couldn't you tried to triage… You tried to save his life. But he was already gone, and you're reliving it in your dreams."

"That's not how it happened."

"You didn't try to save him? You just let him bleed out?"

"*No.* Of course not!" he said, and tacked on a few expletives that let her know how close he was coming to losing control of his temper.

"You tried to treat his wounds but couldn't save him," she summed up instead, her eyes fixed on his hard profile.

It took him a few seconds to respond. "Yes." He glanced at her. "That's your two questions."

She turned in the seat, staring at him longer—and, as much as she actually liked to look at him, it wouldn't help dissipate the negative emotion in the truck. From his answers she could infer that he felt guilt at being unable to save his brother, but trying to save someone in the field was never easy. Sometimes you could stabilize them enough to get transport, but even in a big city with ambulances spread out and close to any location at any time people died before they could get to a hospital all the time.

In a war zone, that level of availability was far-fetched at best.

Would he have felt that way if it hadn't been his brother?

Two questions weren't enough. It didn't give her any real tools that would allow her to help him. And his story didn't jibe with him tackling her and trying to protect her with his body. That wasn't the action of a doctor crippled by the loss of a patient, it was the action of someone who would rather die than lose the person he was trying to protect.

She looked back out the window, and it dawned on her that she'd been sitting, contemplating, brooding, all while looking through the front windshield... Something she never did without panicking.

Paying attention to that brought the fear swimming back, though maybe not as strongly as it had been before. Was the lesser reaction due to her impromptu driving lesson? Or had she just burned through so much emotion since coming to this country that she was becoming numb to it? Maybe it was just the repetition of being in a vehicle over and over while it *didn't* explode... or wreck...or both...

Maybe she could benefit from exposure therapy...

# CHAPTER ELEVEN

THEY ARRIVED IN the new village camp as the sun hit mid-sky and really started to heat up. Since there was no sick child to tend, and because Adalyn really couldn't spend that much time in the super-intense sunlight, she stayed in the truck with the doors open and a book in her hand.

She'd have never pegged Khalil for a fantasy reader, but that's what she found. Epic journeys, men with swords and horses, magic and dragons... Maybe reading was another crutch—though she'd hate to label it so. It could be the kind of escape that took him out of the palace, which she was increasingly certain was what he wanted. She saw him at the palace only when it was time for sleep, and that time got pushed back as far as she'd let it be pushed back before coming to track him down.

By the end of the second chapter the first tent

had been erected—the clinic where Suhail and Hakem also slept at night. She could start carrying in the less heavy pieces, which would still necessitate a walk across the camp at this distance, or she could close the truck up, start it and try to maneuver the thing over to the tent.

She would have to go around, because if she went through she would probably hit and kill someone.

News traveled faster than they did, even between these separated communities. Even though this one was different from the last—and Adalyn believed it was because the people were different even if the tents and configuration all looked remarkably the same to her from the outside—the people had heard the mistress cover story.

She saw it in their eyes when the men looked at her.

Later she'd have to ask Khalil. But for now she approached and touched his arm to get his attention. "If the truck could be moved around to the first tent, I could start unloading some of the supplies."

"Do you want to do it?"

Being generally independent, Adalyn suddenly wanted to say yes. But the more honest answer was no. "I'm afraid I'll hit a tent or a person…" Or that somehow it would go off into the desert at top speed while she tried in vain to stop it. Ridiculous as the idea was. "Will you move it over?"

He nodded, said something to the men and walked back with her to the truck in silence.

That meant she had a small opening to start asking questions. "Are we sharing a tent again?"

Khalil looked down at her and actually smiled, a teasing light in his eyes. "Are you asking to sleep with me?"

Now that they weren't at the palace and she wasn't grilling him about his dreams, his humor had started to come back. No doubt helped by the amount of sleep he'd actually had since the last trip. It was never eight hours, but even a few hours per night was better than what he'd been doing to himself before. And the night she'd woken him…they'd slept more than eight hours afterward, until he had eventually been dragged out of bed to see to some kind of bureaucratic or diplomatic crisis.

Adalyn would've said she was as warm as she could get but, still, with the question and the flirting, she felt her cheeks heat. Yes. Yes, she wanted to sleep with him. "Are you propositioning me?"

"You were propositioning me," he said. "You were the one asking about sleeping together."

"I asked about the tent," she corrected him, but felt herself smiling. "I'll just assume we are. I can't imagine that Hakem or Suhail would want me to crash in their tent."

"I wouldn't be too sure about that, either," he said as they passed a younger village man and watched him eye Adalyn like candy.

The truck sat a few feet away, and she scrambled to it and into the passenger side, letting Khalil get in and get the thing started. "Don't wear your seat belt," he said, stopping her from fastening it.

"Why?"

"We're going a tiny distance."

"Most crashes occur within five miles of home."

"Adalyn, you're trying to overcome your fear of cars, right? Be brave. Take a baby step, and I'll go very slowly around the village. In this flat area I'll make a thirty-second drive take two or three minutes, okay? That's how slow we'll go. So slow that if we managed to hit someone they'd have to be legless and asleep in order to not have time to move out of the way."

She looked at the belt she'd already crossed over her torso and was ready to push into the lock. These little concessions…maybe she could use it as currency again. "For an answer," she said, still holding the warm metal in her hand.

He started the engine and then looked at her, the humor fading a little bit. "Okay, but you sit here beside me, and I get a kiss for my trouble."

"Someone might see…" He was always pushing her boundaries.

"We'll park with the back toward the tent and put up the windshield screen to minimize people seeing…"

Dropping the belt, she slid over on the bench to his side and kept her feet well away from the pedals. Once he got the truck backed up enough to start the creepingly slow trip around to the other tent she asked, "Who were you protecting when you leaped on me in your dream?"

"Arash," he answered, keeping his voice level, though she could see that he was working to hold on to his good mood by the way his knuckles turned white as he gripped the steering wheel.

"But earlier you said you weren't trying to protect him."

"That's not what I said." He peeled one of those white-knuckled hands from the steering wheel and laid it on her knee, squeezed and then slid it between her legs to do the same to her inner thigh.

She was definitely going to sleep with him again. Obviously. They'd been at it a week, but that had been with Khalil, not Zain. This type of behavior felt riskier outside the palace and would require sneakiness she didn't really possess. And patience. They'd have to wait for darkness and the village to get quiet.

But, God help her, the first brush of his fingers on her thighs and her legs actually parted a little to let him do whatever he wanted. It was like watching someone else act, were it not for the inferno that roared to life in her belly—hotter than the sun baking everything and everybody.

By the time they'd made it to the tent she'd forgotten all about the seat belt or her fear. He turned the truck and backed it up to the side of the tent, grabbed the windshield screen, and once that was in place Adalyn's arms shot up to tug his mouth to hers.

Whatever it was that Khalil had, it made her reckless. But it also made her feel alive.

She'd have to think about his answers. Later. After she turned his simple reward kiss into something for him to think about the rest of the day, just as she'd be doing.

And the unspoken agreement she suddenly knew they'd come to.

The early light before dawn had begun to light the tent where Khalil and Adalyn slept.

He lay with her tucked in against him, awake but unwilling to move for the time being. The dream had come, though it hadn't been nearly as bad as before she'd come to Merirach and him.

Yesterday he'd been shorter with her than he'd intended, but he wasn't just putting on a front when he said he didn't know how to talk about the dreams.

Did he need to talk about them? Yes. Even a fool knew that sometimes you had to open a wound and debride it before it could heal. And sometimes an open wound healed better than one that was closed, as contrary to logic as that sounded.

The air was cooler in this part of the small country, and she huddled against him in the bedding, her dark brown tresses fanned out over his arm, which she used as a pillow. Most times when she looked at him it was with the light of challenge in those warm green eyes. Even when it was because he was taking advantage of the peace she brought him. The only time he'd felt even a little peace in the past few months had been since she'd shown up, challenging him.

And sometime over the past ten days her opinion of him had become more important than Jamison's, his closest and longest-standing friend. The man who'd sent this prickly angel to heal him, to keep him sane.

The distinctive bang of a gunshot yanked Khalil out of his reverie and woke his angel.

"What was that?" she asked, sitting up, the sheet clutched to her chest.

He didn't need to ask what it was. He just needed to know why. "Gun. Get dressed." He leaned to the side, grabbed clothes he'd set out the night before and began stuffing himself into them as she did the same.

"Why would anyone be shooting a gun at this time of night?" She looked at the tent canvas and amended, "Morning..."

"No good reason I can think of." One of his lessons from residency had been revived since he'd become regent of Merirach. He knew how to come fully awake and alert fast. "Finish dressing, and stay in the tent. Lie down again on the bedding, low to the ground. I'll check things..."

"Khalil, shouldn't Hakem and Suhail be the ones to check?"

She was worried about him. Well, he was worried about her, too. "It came from that direction."

He pointed toward the center of the village and then looked at her. "If you hear anymore gunshots, take the keys, get into the truck and get out of the village. Do you understand?"

"I'm not leaving you here."

"I'll still have the other truck with Suhail and Hakem. Don't argue for once." He grabbed the keys to the truck and tossed them onto the bed, then exited the tent at a crouching run.

Suhail and Hakem had just come out of the clinic tent, and each man had a gun in hand, ready to defend their prince. He switched to Arabic, since Suhail's English wasn't the greatest. "Do we know what's happening?"

"I heard a disagreement earlier when I made a morning sweep of the village."

Khalil looked at the lightening sky from where the three of them crouched out of view. "Did it sound like it could turn violent?"

"I wasn't expecting it, but these days…"

Another couple of shots sounded and he grunted. "Right. Time to go." He'd have to take it on faith that Adalyn was going to do what he'd told her to do after those other shots.

The three of them moved together, Khalil without a gun, through the winding paths between the tents until they got close enough to hear men arguing over the irregular gunfire.

The next shot came and immediately afterward a woman's screams told him someone had been hit.

"We'll check. You stay here," Hakem said, but Khalil shook his head. He wasn't going to let anyone run off on their own without him again, that lesson he had managed to learn, at least.

"We'll go together."

Several more shots were fired and Khalil swore. The tents were no kind of protection. At least in the capital they'd been able to crouch down behind stone walls and cars to keep from getting shot, but here, even standing out of sight around a tent, a carelessly fired bullet could still slice through layers of canvas and kill him, or anyone else. People in their homes. Children.

The safest option left to him was the one that would ruin his desert forays, but Khalil raised his voice and began to shout who he was. Not Zain. Prince Regent Khalil of Akkari, son of Sultana

Ghada, Daughter of House Merirach. When he'd given his full introduction, he ordered them all to stand down.

All sounds of the argument fell quiet, and the only thing he heard was the sound of the woman crying.

Shrugging off Hakem's attempt to keep him back, Khalil stepped into view, continuing to order the violence to end as he made it to the cleared patch of earth where the men had been fighting. A woman knelt over a downed man, and Khalil stopped beside her to look at the man. He was still conscious, but he had a rapidly expanding red stain on his torso. Hakem followed, and he gestured to the man to apply pressure to the gunshot wound before the man bled out.

It had all happened so quickly—those shots, him blowing his own cover. He had proof back in his belongings if need be…but he hadn't thought to bring any with him when they'd begun chasing gunfire.

People slowly filtered out of their tents to see him for themselves.

"I'm taking him back to get surgery. My men have orders to shoot to kill any citizen who fires another shot while I'm seeing to this man. If it takes violence to end the violence, so be it."

No one argued or demanded proof. No one even dared to speak. But as quickly as it had started, things came to an uneasy calm.

These people who had laughed and joked with him on all his other visits now averted their eyes.

When his mother and aunt had come of age, the culture was different—accepting of a line of succession through the daughters, since the king had no sons. Khalil suspected that situation would've never been questioned had the man who'd married in and become Sultan of Merirach ever tried to earn his people's respect.

But Khalil's line through his mother was of the royal line they'd been ruled by for centuries. They knew her name. He and Malik carried the blood, so they'd accepted her son as the regent and accorded him due respect. The very same reason that those who'd revolted hadn't killed his young cousin, Prince Taariq, even if they'd executed both of his parents.

He left Suhail and Hakem to keep the peace and drafted three men—those who hadn't been fighting—to carry his patient to where he could be treated. Hopefully before it was too late.

Khalil and his entourage rounded the corner to the clinic tent. Adalyn stood outside it, fretting and blatantly disobeying his orders.

The people in the village had obeyed, but she just hadn't been able to do it.

He'd deal with her later.

Yesterday's clinic needs hadn't been sufficient for him to unload the supplies he now needed. They were in the truck. His truck.

Switching to English, he barked at her, "Get into the truck. Get it started."

Then, in the language that the men would understand, he led them to the back of the truck and inside. They placed the man on the floor of the truck and stepped back as Khalil climbed in.

Adalyn was in the front, and she started the engine, as he'd ordered. No arguments, thank God.

"Drive in any direction, Adalyn. I don't care where you take us, just get us out of here."

"Don't you want me to help you?"

"Yes. But I'm not trusting that the people will

hold their truce. Hakem and Suhail are there to keep them peaceful, but the one who shot this man could decide to come and finish him off. I'm not risking your life or his. Just drive."

Adalyn didn't put her seat belt on. She had to back the truck up and get the gears to work, and she'd had only one stupid lesson yesterday when she'd been more concerned with the conversation she hadn't been having with Khalil.

With some grinding of gears she found Reverse and soon they were moving. *Just go straight back, and then when clear of the tents go forward. The lower the number, the lower the gear...* What else? Something about the clutch when she was shifting?

She got the monstrosity moving forward, but she'd be surprised if it didn't need a whole new transmission by the time she got them out of range of the village camp.

When she began to have trouble, Khalil talked her through her nerves, and after they'd been moving a while he called from the back, "Far enough. I need you. Shut it off."

That was easier. Even dealing with surgery

would be better than driving more. She opened the door and climbed down, and then immediately went back inside through the rear door. "Tell me what you need."

"I need…" His pause made her pulse rocket up even higher. Any second and she'd be the one needing help. Opening trunks, she grabbed gloves and some sterile pads. "There are coagulants in the medicine chest. Get those, too. And the dressings."

She watched him turn the man to get a look at his back. "No exit wound."

That was bad. Even she knew that was bad. With the inventory requested tucked under her elbows and the coagulants in hand, she knelt on the other side of his patient, set down the supplies and grabbed the gauze scissors to cut through the man's shirt.

"We need to stop the bleeding. And I want to sedate him, so we need an IV kit. Which—" he looked at the trunks and shook his head "—is in the clinic. So bleeding first."

He wasn't trained as a trauma surgeon, Adalyn knew, he was cardiothoracic by training—just as

Jamison was. But with all the time they'd spent in the field on missions, she could bet that he'd had a good deal of experience with trauma and field surgeries.

As they worked together the tension from the past few minutes slipped away. He alternated between speaking English when it was to give her instructions and Arabic when he spoke to his patient—the man he was trying to keep talking as they worked and, she prayed, stopped him slipping too far into shock.

About ten minutes later they had the bleeding controlled, and their patient was slipping in and out of consciousness. "We have to go back. He's lost a lot of blood, and all I have to give him to hold him over until the chopper comes is saline." He stood, leaving her with the patient. "I'll drive us back. If he exhibits any change, yell."

"Is it safe to go back?"

"We're about to find out," he said, climbing over the seat and into the front, where he started the truck. "Or, actually, I'm about to find out. *You* are going to stay in the truck, like I told you to do before. We're going to have words about that later, Adalyn."

Later. They always had to schedule words for later. At least right now they had more pressing concerns.

When they rolled back into the village the situation seemed to have been brought more or less under control. His men had confiscated the firearms of those who'd been shooting, and they'd stay confiscated until tempers cooled.

Since the situation was more controlled now, Khalil didn't argue when Adalyn asked to go with him and the patient.

As she stood in the tent beside the unconscious man Khalil let her set up the IV and check the man's blood pressure while he stood a short distance away, speaking to a group of several men, the instigators, she'd wager, and Hakem and Suhail.

She gleaned that the men had had some kind of disagreement they wanted Khalil to arbitrate.

And that they no longer called him Zain.

They called him Sheikh. They used honorifics. They bowed, when they weren't quarreling with one another.

Despite the rising heat, her cheeks went cold. They knew.

Khalil stepped over to her with a walkie-talkie, which he tucked into her pocket. "I'm going to go with them, but I won't go far. Call if you need me."

"How'd they find out?" she whispered, looking past him to the men now waiting outside the tent.

A fleeting frown etched between his brows, and he murmured, "I had to tell them who I was in order to stop the shooting. It was the only way to get him out of the line of fire to where we could treat him."

To save a life, he'd given up his haven. No matter what nightmares he was nursing, no matter how caustic and aggressive he could be when confronted with those nightmares, he was an exceptional man. And she had to find a way to help him and get out of there before she lost touch with her life…and what it would be without him in it.

If she didn't leave soon, she'd never want to go.

# CHAPTER TWELVE

BY THE TIME Adalyn heard the helicopter she had just about given up the idea that help was coming. Khalil and his men left her in the clinic with the patient—and his inconsolable wife, she assumed, because communication was impossible.

Moments after she heard the spinning blades beating the air Khalil came back, and soon his men had bundled their patient onto a stretcher and carried him out. "Come on," he said over his shoulder. As little as she wanted to get near another helicopter, she followed. Being in his presence made her feel safe, something she never felt when fending for herself in this country. For all her fears before coming to Merirach, and all that she'd worked through in the meanwhile to get the job done, being alone and unable to communicate with anyone was quickly becoming a big enough fear to compete with vehicles.

The sun had well and truly risen now, and as she stepped out of the shade of the tent the heat on her head and neck baked into her, and she had to scramble to keep up.

Burning, stinging sand whipped through the air from the force of the propeller blades as the chopper landed. Her lungs reacted with a coughing fit that stopped her cold. Why did he need her to go to the helicopter anyway? She could stand a safe distance away and wait for him.

She turned away from the dust, which helped a little.

Khalil couldn't have heard her coughing above that blade, but he must have sensed that she'd stopped. In an instant he was at her side with a cloth to hold over her mouth so she could breathe and his insistent arm around her shoulders, guiding her toward the chopper.

The closer they got to it the better it got, but before she knew what was happening he'd grabbed her by the hips and put her into the helicopter.

"Wait…" She pulled the cloth away from her face, forcing her eyes open to look at him.

"You have to go with him."

Go without Khalil? Far from his presence? Alone? The barren landscape behind him seemed to spin. Was it because of the coughing she'd been doing and the drop in oxygen saturation? Or was it the mountain of fear pressing at her chest?

Adalyn grabbed his hands to keep him from getting away. "Please, don't make me go in the helicopter. I want to stay! You need help!" Even as the words came out she knew how desperate she sounded.

"I have Hakem and Suhail."

"I can't go to some whole other place without you. I don't speak the language!" He had to know how much the idea scared her. He'd been with her nearly two weeks now, and more than a few of her neurotic fears had manifested in that time.

"They're going to the hospital to take him to surgery, and then they'll take you to the palace. I have to stay and clean up this mess."

Did he always sound so distant? There wasn't even a hint of playful flirting or even gentleness in his eyes as he said the words, ignoring her pleas.

She couldn't think of a suitable argument other than that she didn't want to. All she managed was to shake her head. "I'll stay in the truck, I'll wait in the truck."

"I need you gone, Adalyn," he shouted over the beating blades, then pulled her head to his mouth to say, "You're my mistress…"

And then it all became clear. The people in this village knew who he was, and they believed her to be his mistress. And she didn't even know if that was inaccurate anymore, but this had become somewhere possibly not safe for her.

There was no argument for this situation. She nodded dully and edged back into a seat to buckle in. What would she find when she got to the palace? Would his staff be willing to accept her without him at her side? Did they look upon her as his mistress, too? They'd not done an especially good job of hiding the turn their relationship had taken over the past week, even if right now it all felt like her nightmares…more emotion than substance, some kind of fantasy she'd played out in her head.

They'd happily slept in his bed, and she knew those details...the scent of his rumpled sheets, the way the morning sun hit the east windows and little shafts of light peeked past the heavy curtains and turned his warm tan skin to gold. She could barely remember the bed in her suite—it had sat untouched since her first night in Merirach.

Details that made it real.

In a remarkably short period of time the men had all retreated to a safe distance and the helicopter began to lift. Unlike the last time, she didn't avoid looking out the window.

Details she could remember later, and know this was also real. The way the helicopter smelled slightly of fuel and fumes, the feel of the headphones thrust into her hands and soon cushioning her ears. The way Khalil marched back to the village without a backward glance.

This was real. He could just send her away without it putting even a small chink in his armor. Without worrying about her or dreading her absence.

Because it wasn't nighttime. He didn't need his crutch unless it was time to sleep…

If she'd wondered what his feelings for her were before, she now knew.

She was the only fool who'd managed to fall in love.

Emotionally battered from the turn the day had taken, by the time Adalyn reached the palace all she wanted to do was climb into her neglected bed.

No, if she was honest, she wanted to climb into Khalil's bed. She wanted to burrow into his sheets, press her face in his pillow and breathe in the last of him. Whatever they'd been, it certainly felt over.

The car from the airport pulled into the palace, and she got out. Exposure therapy was definitely working for her. After the nightmare of a helicopter ride she'd had a remarkably dull reaction to yet another wheeled vehicle to spirit her to the palace.

As soon as she stepped out, dread prickled at

the back of her neck. The man who managed the house staff stood alone to receive her.

"Hello…" she said, gesturing to the car. "The sheikh isn't with me. He—"

"I am aware, Miss Quinn. Your suite has been prepared," he said, but then looked uncertain for a moment before he lowered his voice. "Sultan Khaliq Al-Akkari has arrived with the Sultana Ghada. They await the return of their son."

Adalyn blinked, and the emotion that had left her for the drive up to the palace came roaring back. Did she need to talk to them? Was she supposed to explain where Khalil was?

"Do you know why they've come?"

"I do not," he answered, but had the look of a man not used to lying. He knew. Adalyn would stake her passport on it.

But she couldn't very well call the man a liar. And she also couldn't count on him to give her good advice on how to handle this situation.

"I suppose I will go clean the grit off myself and then go meet them."

"Very good," he said, turning to lead her to her suite, as if she didn't know how to get there. He felt more like a prisoner escort than something for her benefit.

"Do they know that I'm…?"

"They know everything."

Great. They knew everything, and she didn't even know what her reaction was supposed to be, or if she was supposed to try to smooth things over before Khalil got there.

She passed through Khalil's bedroom. All her equipment still littered the suite, but when she passed the camera stand a wave of cold crept over her scalp and down her spine.

The tripod remained, but the base where her camera had sat? Empty. No camera.

And she hadn't touched it since the only night of proper monitoring…

She hadn't had the focus to remember it was recording and turn it off when he'd taken her to bed. Or when he'd stripped her clothes off, torn wires and electrodes off his own body and kissed her senseless.

The only video on that camera started out with Khalil sleeping and ended with a night-vision capture of the two of them sleeping together.

* * *

No sooner had Khalil returned to the village after sending away Adalyn than his satellite phone rang.

Only his parents, his minsters and staff had the number to the phone.

He glanced at the number calling and let it go to voice mail. He'd already rung his head of staff to let him know that Adalyn was returning and to arrange transport for her back to the palace, and she couldn't be there yet. He had a little time, and he had to deal with the situation that had prompted a sunrise shooting before he could do one more thing.

Within the next hour he gathered all the men together, decided who had the best reputation among the people and appointed an official to hear these sorts of disagreements and resolve them peacefully. How would that work out? He had no idea. The lessons in leadership he'd had growing up had never really centered around bureaucratic issues. Arash's had. Malik's had, too. But they had been the ones meant to lead. He was just an extra spare who'd messed up the line of succession when he'd let his brother die. All he could do was use his best judgment, and hope it was a better judgment now than it had been two months ago.

As Hakem and Suhail worked with the village men to pack up the tent and supplies, Khalil adjourned to the truck to return the call.

The voice that answered…

"Father…" he said, his mind whirring now as he looked at his watch and started calculating the time it took to fly home versus how long ago he'd sent Adalyn off.

She was there by now, God help them both.

There was no way for her to stay with him now, unless his father took the tack he expected—the one that removed him from the regent position and replaced him with Malik.

He'd be failing Arash for a third time if he lost the regency, forced his father out of retirement and his elder brother to clean up his mess…

And the day had started out so well, when it had been just her lying in his arms, looking like an angel…

But he couldn't fail again. Even if that meant losing Adalyn.

When it came down to it, he didn't deserve her light anyway.

Adalyn lay in the bed in her suite, staring at the carved floral reliefs on the ceiling, an untouched dinner tray sitting on the table beside her.

After showering and making herself presentable, the sultan and sultana had refused to see her.

They hadn't even wanted to meet her, and she was so mortified about the missing camera that she couldn't even bring herself to try to sweet-talk her way in to see them—if she even knew how to sweet-talk.

Another new experience she could add to her own personal travelogue.

She hadn't visited ancient monuments…unless the palace counted, but it didn't look all that ancient.

She hadn't gone to the beach.

She hadn't gone on any fancy shopping sprees, hadn't even gone to some chintzy souvenir shop.

Despite the initial rockiness, by the time they'd made it to the first village Khalil had made her part of his daily life, part of his obligations...

And then there were the other things she'd done that you couldn't really put into the travelogue.

Fallen in love with the regent of a country? Yeah, that was probably not fit for publishing.

Accidentally made a sex tape with her patient, the same regent? That was also right out.

Had they watched it? Was that why they wouldn't see her? Would it be better or worse if the sultan had it, or if one of the staff had taken it to later blackmail Khalil with?

She'd come reluctantly to the Middle East, then had sullied her name among the people as a— well, she wasn't sure what they thought of the word *mistress*, but, considering how distasteful she found it with her liberal Western upbringing, she could only imagine.

This was exactly why she should've just stuck with her travel books. The next time Jamison came calling to make her travel to help out one of his friends she'd—well, she'd say something rude and then slam the door in his face. Or the phone in his ear, as most of their communication happened on the phone.

She felt Khalil standing there more than anything else. The door didn't squeak. The floor didn't squeak. The plush rugs on the floor also muffled footfalls remarkably well.

"Someone took the camera," she said immediately, bolting upright. He looked dirty and exhausted from the road, and now he had to face all this insanity at the palace. "I'm sorry. I should have said hello first." Pulling herself up from the bed, she covered the few feet separating them but couldn't bring herself to touch him. The fear that she was alone in these new emotions might have been worse than the fear she'd felt getting into the helicopter.

Khalil didn't touch her but lifted a hand to rub the back of his neck, then turned to prowl to the window. Did he not even want to look at her?

Suddenly trying to figure out how he felt about her seemed like the most important thing, more important than the camera or the publicity debacle. Before he'd sent her away she'd have said he felt the same, but in that moment—when he'd excluded her from his life and obligations—any sense of security had vanished. She'd just given him an opportunity to remedy that—one small touch would've done it. Or at least gone a long way toward doing it, and he'd walked away.

"Say something. Please, say anything."

With his voice bouncing off the glass, he said, "I'm here to take you to the airport."

"What?"

"You're going home."

"Because your parents wouldn't see me? Because of the missing camera?"

"No…"

The way the word hung there she knew it to be a lie. Of course the camera mattered. Of course his parents had seen it. Once again that cold settled into her spine as heat washed over her face. A body at war over how to feel, embarrassed or scared?

"What does that mean? Are we… Are we breaking up?"

"What did you think was going to happen when you had to go home?" Khalil asked, finally turning to look at her. Those beautiful golden-brown eyes now looked hard, like sharp bits of glass ready to slash at her. That she was even making an argument about their relationship was like handing him her wrists or exposing her jugular.

"I don't know. We haven't even tried to figure it out. We could do that. There has to be something. Isn't that what you're supposed to do when you love someone? Work it out? Be together…?" There, she'd said it. She'd said *love*. She'd taken that brave first step. All he had to do was…

"It was never going to work out."

"It could," she said, trying to ignore that he hadn't denied he loved her. He hadn't confirmed it, either, but he still could. "It should. It's supposed to work out. That's how this goes in the stories, when two people—good people—find each other, it's supposed to work out. They're supposed to make it work."

"What makes you think I'm a good person?"

The question sounded so ridiculous to her that it took Adalyn a moment to even figure out if she was supposed to answer it. Was he so eager to get rid of her that he'd say anything? She already knew that she was weak enough to say anything to avoid it.

"I know you're a good person. I see the way you take care of your people. I'm a good person, too."

"I'm not a good person. I'm not the hero here, I'm the villain who should never have won the crown, let alone the woman. I'm not one of your dream warriors. Adalyn. I'm the dragon."

It always came back to that, to the nightmare that he never shared.

"Why do you say these things about yourself? You wanted to save him, Khalil. You wanted to and you're still trying. Every night." Or the nights when he hadn't been with her. The nights he'd spent alone with his grief and his penance...

"I didn't try to save him." He blurted the words out, all but yelling them as he stormed for her. "I killed him." The words came out sharp and hard, and when he finally touched her it was with cold hands gripping her shoulders just a little too tight. "Is that real enough for you? You want to make things work with a man who killed his brother for power?"

"I don't believe you," she whispered, mentally replaying everything he'd said to her about his brother.

"Why? You think you're going to redeem me with the power of love?"

In all her interactions with Khalil she'd seen him sad, she'd seen him happy, she'd seen duty and caring on his face. She'd seen stubbornness and authority. But she'd never seen him like this. She'd never heard such malice in his voice. With his hands still gripping her shoulders, she lifted her own to cup his jaw, making him look at her.

"I don't have to redeem you," she said, but she was already starting to doubt. Maybe she didn't know him. Maybe all that she'd thought she'd learned about him was a front, a disguise. Maybe she had fallen for Zain, not Khalil… But she wasn't ready to believe that, either. If he was sending her away, she'd have the truth first at the very least. "I already know you too well to think that's necessary. If you killed your brother, tell me why. What was your motive?"

He let go of her so he could pull back far enough to be out of reach, breaking the small contact she'd felt blooming beneath her palm. But in the wake of it, if anything, he seemed angrier. "Jealousy. I wanted to lead. But they already had an heir and a spare, they didn't need me. I was never meant to reign, but I wanted to. That's why."

She'd come here scared of her own shadow, someone who avoided knowing others, who avoided pain and danger, but she was now ready to fight. "You wanted to be regent, that's what you're saying? You killed Arash so they'd be forced to send you here instead?"

"Why else?" He threw his arms in the air, the look on his face tortured and angry, but beneath that she could see a plea—that she save him from it somehow.

That look was the only thing that kept her going. "That's such a lie. You regent as little as you can before you escape back into the desert. For a man who thinks he wants to lead, you spend a heck of a lot of time running from it."

"Because of the nightmares."

"No. You're lying to yourself. Stop blaming the nightmares!" She grabbed his hand again, needing to touch him, needing him to feel her hand in his—as if by touching him she could help him see what she saw. That the feeling that always raced through her body would be mirrored in his, because it was love. It was love and she needed him to know it.

"This is about you. You could go into the desert and not treat anyone if you simply wanted to get away from the palace. There's a whole wide desert out there where you could hide in a tent with that satellite phone for emergencies and read. Or you could shun responsibility and go off to some fancy hotel and find some woman who's actually good at being a trollop, and let her soothe your tortured royal brow. But you don't. You go into the desert to help people. You take care of them."

"I take terrible care of them. I make bad decisions."

"Only when you're sleep-deprived. And you suffer for those bad decisions."

"Stop trying to make me the good guy!" He wrenched his hand from her touch again, throwing up walls. And every one made it harder for her to keep fighting. "And, since we're on the subject, stop tearing down your own skills as a trollop. You did a fine job."

Adalyn's newly freed hand flew, her palm connecting with his cheek before either of them seemed to know it was going to happen. His head snapped back but he didn't move away. Didn't touch her. Didn't do anything but stare at her, any trace of love she might have imagined during their tender moments…gone. Just gone.

Her chest burned, along with her palm and her eyes. At any second her heart would tear itself from her chest.

She'd be the one to walk away this time. If she didn't, she might hit him again. Or he might touch her and that connection she all but lived for would turn sour, and it might take all the sand in the desert to fill her chest back up.

"You're not a dragon," she muttered. "You might be mean enough when you want to be, but dragons aren't cowards. Get out so I can pack."

"You don't need to. I'll have it all packed and sent to you on a separate flight."

Right. He couldn't even let her have enough

time to pack, he wanted her gone that badly. Had the sultan ordered her out of the country? Or was this entirely Khalil's doing?

Whatever. It didn't matter whose idea it was, the result was the same. "Don't strain yourself. I can live without it for a few days. But if you're looking for a good use of your time, see if you can find your courage, because you need to figure out what really happened. Talk to someone. If not your family, then talk to Jamison."

She put her shoes on, grabbed her purse to make sure that her passport and keys were inside and gestured for him to go.

"I could say the same thing to you."

"You could, but it would be redundant. I'm already going to. The world's biggest scaredy-cat has more courage than you. Live with that."

She wouldn't say goodbye. Even if she wanted to, she doubted another word could get past her lips without making her sick.

There had never been a longer day in Khalil's life. A fresh stone of guilt had sat putrefying in his middle since he'd said those ugly words to

Adalyn. Even the small amount of pride he'd felt when she'd slapped him for the ugly lie wasn't enough to help.

Not bothering to clean up or to change into the robes his position required, Khalil headed to his parents' suite and through the double doors. Behind him, flanking him on either side, were Hakem and Suhail, his ever-present escorts. Who, technically, worked for his father.

Despite the violence that the palace had seen only two months earlier, it had been well reordered. A few bullet holes still pitted the walls here and there, but you had to know where to look for them. It had mostly been put right now. The furniture that had been irreparable had been replaced. The evidence of the repairs greeted him: a large-screen television with the eerie, frozen, night-vision-green image of him sleeping, covered in wires and electrodes, his limbs caught in mid-motion and his sleeping face contorted. Nightmare face. Beside him, Adalyn stood, hand outstretched, ready to wake him.

His parents sat on a sofa together, always together, reading a newspaper and paying no attention to the television. But only a second after he stepped in they looked toward him and his entourage.

Khalil stepped forward, bowed deeply, as he'd been taught, and straightened. Get it over with. A quick glance around confirmed that his elder brother would be back in Akkari—he was now running the country full-time, since his father had decided to step back and ostensibly retire, to spend more time with his wife. Which was why Malik wasn't the regent of Merirach, and it had fallen to Arash previously, and then Khalil.

Without speaking a word, his father reached for the remote and set the video playing.

When Khalil didn't look anywhere but at his father he said, "Look at the video, son."

Son?

He didn't need to look. He knew what had happened next. He just didn't know why his father would want to play it, except to drive home the notion that he'd let them all down, and then... sullied the palace by bringing in a lover. It was the fact that Adalyn would soon be nude on that screen that put him into motion.

Three big steps and he made it to his father, took the remote and stopped the video just at the beginning of his leap from the bed, which had ended with him tackling her and…

"I don't need to see this. She doesn't deserve to be shamed."

"That's not what we're going to look at, Khalil," his mother said, and he met her gaze for the first time. Tears wet her eyes.

"There's nothing else to see," he whispered, and stepped back, keeping his head up even if his will to fight was fading.

"You were having sleep disturbances," his father said, avoiding any wording that would make the situation more personal or emasculating. Something he'd be grateful for if he had an ounce of feeling left to spare. "You had her here to help you."

"Yes."

"She woke you and you leaped on her."

"Yes."

"Just as you screamed for your brother to come back."

Khalil opened his mouth to say yes, but then

frowned and looked back at the frozen screen. He didn't remember shouting anything.

This wasn't about his lie to the people that Adalyn was his mistress, and it wasn't about his secret trips into the desert under a different identity or shirking responsibility.

They wanted to talk about the dream, not what had come after the tackle.

That was really the way he'd let his family and his country down.

Khalil looked at the remote in his hand…found the button and pressed Play.

# CHAPTER THIRTEEN

ADALYN STOOD IN her apartment, the upper floor of an old Victorian that had been widely refurbished since Hurricane Katrina, staring at her bookshelf.

So many travel books.

A stranger would look at her bookcase and think she'd traveled the world, but Jamison was the world traveler.

She was just the kid sister who read about all the countries he traveled to.

Initially, she'd done this to understand the sorts of dangers he could encounter so she could warn him of all the things he needed to watch out for. He wouldn't have done that research on his own after all.

But somewhere along the way it had become a way for her to see the world without leaving home. Some way to scratch that itch to know more. She had books about places Jamison had never gone. They might even outnumber the ones she'd had a real reason to purchase, at least by her way of thinking.

It had started out noble and had turned into something sad without her even realizing it.

The people at the bookstore knew it was strange. They'd always asked questions designed to lead her to the same conclusion—not-so-subtle hints for her to actually go somewhere that she'd always understood but had viewed through the lenses of *Other People's Opinions* and everyone being entitled to theirs. Even if they were wrong.

Her reading proclivities had seemed entirely normal and rational to her before Merirach.

Now her life seemed small. And what she'd once deemed safe? Lonely.

Jamison would be there soon, and she had to figure out what to tell him about all this, but she didn't even know where to start.

She'd been home for eight long, rainy days now, and it suited her mood. A mood she couldn't hide, which was why her brother was coming for a second in-person visit in as many months. She'd been dodging his calls since she'd gotten home.

Apparently texts hadn't been enough to put his mind at ease.

So, what could she tell him to explain things without involving the whole mistress affair or the accidental sex tape? If her current mood had been because of any man other than his best friend, she'd just tell him the truth. Everything, save for the sexy details. Straightforward. Honest.

The doorbell rang and she got a sinking feeling in her stomach. If she wasn't going to tell him about Khalil, she should finally tell him about her nightmares. *Straightforward* and *honest* weren't really words she could claim for their relationship for the past fifteen or so years.

And that had to change.

She drew a deep breath and went to answer the door. Time to follow her own advice and talk to her family about her problems. Let her big brother look out for her for once...

Jamison unfolded another sturdy banker's box and set it beside Adalyn where she sat cross-legged on the floor.

"You know, I want to keep some of these," she said, looking at the piles of travel guides circling her. "I've sorted them. Those are the ones that will be donated for sure. These are the ones I want to keep—the ones I think I'll use."

Jamison lifted a brow and squatted down beside her. "When?"

"Sometime…"

His brow rose higher.

"Sometime soon." She tried again.

He turned and sat cross-legged on the floor opposite her, the books piled between them. "I'm sorry, the judges won't accept that answer. When?"

She groaned. In the five days since her confession Jamison's interest in her general homebody tendencies had become extremely annoying, but it was her fault. She was the one who'd told him she responded to exposure therapy…because of that stupid truck.

"All right. How about this? You pick the place you're going to go to first, and then we'll start working on when. Seasons matter in travel." He picked up the books from the rejects pile and put them into the box. "And tomorrow we're going to the amusement park."

"No, we're not." She stopped looking at the books, trying to figure out a city to go to. One within the United States. Maybe one she could get to by train. A good train adventure sounded like just the thing. They hardly ever crashed, unless it was wintertime. Or maybe if there was an earthquake.

So maybe she shouldn't go west…

"Two words," he said, holding up his closed hand. "Bumper. Cars." He ticked off the words by extending fingers.

Adalyn smiled and then laughed a little. "I don't think that's necessary."

"You're going. Whether you want to or not."

"I really don't think I have a problem with amusement park rides."

"Good. You're going." He looked at the maybe pile. "You have to pick so I can pack them up."

The doorbell rang, buying her a little more time. "I think your pizza is here."

"God, I hope so." He levered himself off the floor and left her to look at her books.

At least him fixating on her exposure therapy was better than him continuing to grill her about what had gone on between her and Khalil. She'd managed not to say anything up to this point, which was why she'd definitely give in and go to the stupid park tomorrow. It might save their friendship.

She went through the maybe pile again, considering each destination and whatever local attractions she could remember from whenever she'd read the book. This resulted in five more books being plucked out of it to go into the donation box, neatly dividing the maybe stack in half.

Then it occurred to her. She went through the stack of books before Jamison could get his pizza at the front door, maybe thirty steps away, flight of stairs included?

She stood up and went to the door. Jamison was not at the bottom of the stairs. Pizza nowhere in sight. No delivery person, either.

A worrier couldn't learn to stop worrying overnight. After double-checking to make sure the door wouldn't lock behind her, she trotted down the stairs and out onto the porch.

Jamison stood, holding his right hand protectively.

A few feet away a man lay sprawled on his back.

"You hit the pizza dude?" she barked at him as she slowly processed the scene.

Only then the pizza dude sat up, and it was Khalil.

Khalil was on her front porch. Without pizza. But he did have blood on his mouth and cheek.

The air felt even soupier than normal suddenly, and she had to force deep slow breaths if she wanted any chance of keeping that fear-tinged hopefulness from showing. He'd knocked the air out of her before, but really she'd prefer a tackle.

"Why in the world would you hit Khalil?" she shouted at Jamison, but didn't move toward either man.

"Because he messed with you. You mess with your best friend's sister, you take a punch. It's simple math," Jamison said, now shaking his hand out, as if that would dispel the smarting.

"I didn't tell you anything that happened between us."

"You didn't have to," Jamison muttered. "You've been inexplicably teary-eyed at different times of the day since I got here. I might be dense sometimes, but I know heartache when I see it."

There simply was no argument to be made against that. Her eyes burned, that inexplicable teariness threatening to return. She muttered, "For all your insight, you probably broke a knuckle, Einstein." When she transferred her attention to Khalil, though, words completely failed her.

"It's okay. It's fair," Khalil said, defending the man who'd probably just split his lip, and slowly climbed back to his feet.

Behind him, down on the street, the delivery car pulled up, finally giving her something else to focus on. She turned her attention back to Jamison and snapped her fingers. "Wallet. Then go upstairs. Both of you. I'll get the stupid pizza."

The transaction took no time at all. She took the money from the wallet, handed it to the young female driver, apologized for the chaos and then stood on the porch for a couple of minutes, box in hand.

Khalil was there. Upstairs. In her apartment.

And he hadn't looked as if he'd come to see Jamison.

She stood there, staring at the front door, until her heart slowed into something resembling a normal rhythm.

It had been two weeks and she'd just gotten to the place where, as Jamison had said, she wasn't inexplicably teary at different points throughout the day. Today it had happened only twice.

If the wound had been physical, she'd have said it had finally begun to heal. But it wasn't strong. A stiff gulf breeze could break those stitches.

And she was taking as long to get the pizza as she'd thought Jamison had.

*Just go upstairs. Get it over with...*

She pushed through the door and with slow, measured steps climbed to her apartment door.

Khalil stood in the middle of the living room, a paper towel held to his lip, waiting for Adalyn when every inch of him wanted to go make sure she was coming.

To control the instinct, he looked at his best friend on the couch, a bag of frozen vegetables on his knuckles.

"She's probably right," Khalil said, trying to ignore the lump in his throat he just couldn't swallow down.

"About?"

"Your hand. It's at least sprained."

"I'll be fine." Jamison said, smirking up at him in a way that relieved at least a tiny bit of his tension. "Your face is soft like a pretty-pretty princess. Couldn't have done too much damage."

Khalil laughed, a small nod to hope—hope that the other Quinn was as quick to forgive. She certainly wasn't as quick to come back upstairs.

By the time the door opened Khalil had given up waiting and started forward to go to check on her. They met at the door.

"Are you leaving?" she asked, glancing up long enough to make eye contact, and then stepped around him.

"I... No." He didn't explain, just waited as she

took the last few steps to Jamison. "Not until I say what I came to say."

She thrust the wallet and the pizza at Jamison and said, "Don't eat this in my living room." When she had been relieved of her cargo she looked back at Khalil.

If she wanted to do this in front of Jay, he'd do it. He'd faced down his parents, he could do this.

Even if he got an ulcer afterward from the acid eating through his stomach.

He stood straighter.

She didn't look at him again, just gestured for him to follow her and headed back out of the living room in another direction.

They came to a simple white-paneled door and she held it for him.

Bedroom. He knew what it was before he even got through the door to see. It smelled of her so strongly that a wave of homesickness unlike anything he'd ever experienced slammed into him.

Instinct said to go to the window, look out, compose himself... Protect his emotions. He'd done that before to her, until he'd gotten control. But this couldn't be about control. It had to be real.

He swallowed, and though his eyes felt damp he turned to look at her. She stood close enough that he could have touched her. He wanted to touch her. Skip the words, take her to bed, let his body say what he was uncertain his words could.

The small tan she'd picked up in Merirach had faded with her days home, freckles had come out on the bridge of her nose and a smattering on her cheeks…almost the exact color of the desert sand. Close enough that he had to fight the urge to run his thumb over her cheeks to brush them clean.

She looked down again so that her dark hair fell forward and concealed her eyes from him. "You have to talk. I don't know what to say."

He stuffed his hands into his pockets to keep from reaching for her. "I need to talk to you about the camera."

"I don't have it…" She breathed the words in a rush, her eyes lifting with her hands as she shrugged. "I don't have any of it. The equipment isn't here yet."

"I brought it with me," he said. "It's at the airport, awaiting delivery instructions."

"So the memory card…"

"I…" He withdrew his hands from his pockets, opened his jacket and fished out the small blue card and held it out to her. "That's it."

She didn't reach for it but stared at it hard, probably to keep from looking at him. "Don't you want to destroy it?"

"No. I want it. I'm hoping that you'll let me keep it. That we can…we can keep it." Together. He should say that. Together.

It was enough to get her to make eye contact again. For the moment the look of imminent tears was replaced with a spark of the sass and sarcasm he'd missed in her. "It's that good, eh? You think I want a copy to remember you by?"

"No." He swallowed, still holding it out to her. "I'm hoping that you'll let me keep it as a record of…my journey."

Adalyn looked at the card but looked harder at the way his hand shook. Fear? Nerves? "Your journey? What journey?"

He dropped his hand down, curling the card back into his palm as he shook his head.

"That's not the right word, but it sort of is," he said, "because it shows where I was before I met you, and where I want my life to end. This video could be my whole story." He paused to swallow.

The vulnerability in his voice nearly undid her. At any second now the tears she worked to keep at bay would spring forth again. "I don't mean to be dense, I just don't—"

"Adalyn Quinn woke me up from my nightmare, and I loved her for the rest of my life," Khalil said, cutting off her question. "That's what I want my story to be. Because my whole life was a nightmare when I met you. It just got easier to recognize as a nightmare when I was sleeping."

Her chest constricted and no amount of willpower could keep away the tears burning her eyes. She gave up fighting them and simply reached up to swipe them away. It couldn't be that easy. It was never that easy. He ran a country. A faraway country… "But what about our lives being too different?"

"Shouldn't we try to figure it out? That's what people do when they're in love."

He'd used the words she'd said to him, so he *had* been listening, and he'd remembered. It would be so easy to say yes, and inside her the word echoed and bounced off her heart, but she still ached from the last time she'd opened herself up to him. Every day. All the time…

"Because I love you," he added.

*Don't listen to that. Not yet.*

"But your people think I'm a brazen harlot," she said, and then remembered. "Your parents! Your parents think—"

"My parents only watched the first part of the video, until my mother realized what was going on. Then she turned it off and explained the situation to my father. She said it's what young people do in the West when they're in love. Apparently my mother thinks sex tapes are all the rage. Like digital engagement rings."

She'd never even met them, but the little story tickled her. Adalyn covered her mouth, hope surging through her at the twinkle of amusement in his eyes. But he sobered quickly enough to remind her that this wasn't a joke. It was everything important.

"It was the first part of the recording they were concerned about."

Yes. His sleep study. The tackle. Him trying to protect Arash… Words she was still desperate to hear. Dropping her hand, she shifted a half step closer to him. "Your nightmares?"

"And what I said when I leaped on you." Khalil nodded, holding his hand out to her again with the memory card on his palm, still offering it to her. But she'd definitely have to touch him to take it, and there were things she had to know first. She had to be safe.

"I didn't understand what you said, and I didn't remember enough of what it sounded like later to look it up."

"It was a warning. For Arash. I'd seen the man with the gun pop up from behind a car and take aim at him." He rubbed his upper lip, a nervous fidget.

"So you tried to get him to take cover?"

He nodded.

"So you didn't kill him."

He shook his head. "When I heard what I'd shouted it triggered a memory. Like you said, a memory with more detail than my dreams. I've been working on it. Made a timeline. Wrote it down... Am still writing down any details as they come to me. But I don't think I'm in remission yet. The nightmares still come, not every time I sleep but they're still there. Even though I'm out of the palace now. The change in sleep environment might be what's helping, or the memory details I'm getting back. I'm not sure which."

He was out of the palace. Did that mean he could stay here?

"Did they fire you?" Adalyn swallowed and took another step, close enough that his clean masculine scent wrapped around her like a hug. Every word strengthened that feeling. If she didn't get hold of herself, she was going to either lean against him and sob...or leap on him and kiss his split lip.

"Fire me?"

"Your parents. From being the regent?"

"Ah. I believe it would be closer to medical

leave. My father has a greater capacity for compassion than I gave him credit for. He stepped back into active leadership of Akkari so Malik could go to Merirach in my place. Because…I need help with this."

If she breathed too deeply, his fingertips would press against her breasts, but there it was, that card still settled on his palm between them, hers for the taking.

Adalyn leaned back enough to wrap his hand in both of hers, then curled his fingers back over the card. "So you were thinking of staying for a while?"

"And about begging you to tell me…" His words trailed off and he had to take two breaths before he could finish his thought. "Tell me I didn't break us in a way that couldn't be mended."

Adalyn felt another rush of tears on her cheeks, and before she could reach for them he lifted his other hand and ran the pad of his thumb under one of her eyes.

She wanted to lean into his hand but managed to speak first. "You didn't. But we still have some things to work out." Several, but none of them seemed quite so pressing as kissing him right now. "Which we should do. Later," she said, finally letting go of his hand so she could fling her arms around his neck.

He caught her with both arms, squeezing her to him as his mouth came down on hers, heedless of the split in his lip.

Unlike in his bedroom, Khalil couldn't navigate hers with his eyes closed. His arms still tight around her, he lifted until her feet left the floor, broke the kiss just long enough to orient himself and returned his lips to hers.

Unlike the first time he'd carried her to bed, and despite the need she knew was coiling in him as it did in her, he followed her onto the pillowed duvet and slowed everything down. No need-fueled rush to completion, just kissing for the sake of kissing. Thorough. Playful. Loving.

Hungry and devastating, anointed by the coppery ping of his blood and the salt of her tears but somehow still sweet and full of promises.

"I don't hear any arguing in there!" The sound of her irritating brother's shouted words filtered through the door. Adalyn chuckled against his lips and Khalil leaned up enough to look at her as they shared a smile, both shaking their heads.

When they didn't answer, another shout came. "If you're having sex, I'm gonna have to burn the house down! Just sayin'."

They both laughed for real then and called back in unison, "Shut up, Jamison!"

As she breathed him in, a wave of peace washed over her and she could almost hear the dunes in her ears. The sound of all that sand she'd packed that hole in her chest with draining away, and something altogether sweeter refilling her.

If he was brave enough to face those nightmares haunting him, come to find her and take a punch from her brother but still remain friends, he was the kind of man worth fighting for. Her faith in him had never been misplaced, even when she'd doubted.

Khalil was her oasis. Her safe place.

Everything else they could work out.

Because that's what two people did when they loved each other…even if they had to ban Jamison from the house until then.

# EPILOGUE

ADALYN AL-AKKARI SAT in a window seat in one of the family planes, the seat belt stretched around the swell of her belly.

It had been seven months since she'd flown home, her heart in tatters, on that very same jet. But this flight was different; this time Khalil sat beside her, his hand in hers.

"Breathe through it, love," Khalil said, alerting Adalyn to how hard she was gripping his hand.

From across the aisle Jamison laughed. "Get used to saying that. You have two more months to practice. Though I expect it's more likely that you'll say it once and then pass out while Adalyn and I deliver that baby."

A quick chuckle was all Adalyn could spare for her brother's antics. Teasing them—but Khalil especially—never got old for him. Even after they'd exchanged vows and she'd got a new, exotic last name, and a lot better at traveling.

But descent still had the ability to scare her.

"I'm delivering the baby," Khalil countered, not rising to Jamison's baiting for once, though she could still hear the amusement in his voice contrasting with the tenderness he channeled to her through the slow back-and-forth motion of his thumb on her hand. Steady. Strong. Comforting. Protective. "Besides, you're going to be too busy traveling to the camps to be there for the birth. We'll send you a picture, though, on the satellite phone."

"Then I hope it looks like me. You want a handsome kid."

Not long after Khalil had shown up on her doorstep, even before his lip had healed from Jamison's punch, she'd realized their desert shenanigans had produced a baby. And for some reason birth was one thing she wasn't afraid of.

Khalil resuming his regency? That could cause her a little flare of nerves... But he'd come so far that even the sultan and his elder brother believed Khalil ready to return to his position. And, more important, Khalil felt ready, too.

The nightmares had grown infrequent for both of them, but when they flared up neither of them needed a CD to coax them back into peaceful slumber. Instead, they took turns whispering words of healing comfort to one another in that suggestible period of early slumber, and it worked even better.

Five years wasn't so long to serve the people and do right by his family. He needed to do it, and she needed it for him. In a few years, the young heir would finish school and come of age, and they could return to practice, along with the many children she'd decided in the past few months she wanted. A huge family, with as many people to love and worry about as she could manage. Jamison had even agreed to spend at least a year taking over the mobile practice Khalil had started, so she'd even have her often absent brother near her.

The plane set smoothly down and Adalyn breathed her way through the landing and taxiing to the recently reopened terminal at Merirach's airport.

No more living through books and travelogues. No more hiding herself away to stay safe.

But she would wait until the plane stopped to unfasten her seat belt.

* * * * *